LynnVisible

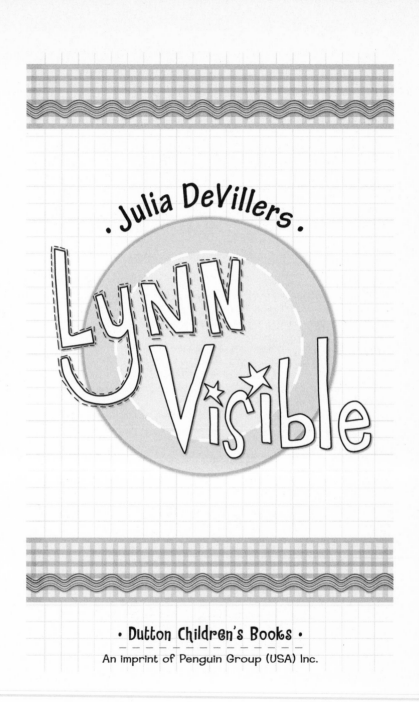

· Julia DeVillers ·

LYNN Visible

· Dutton Children's Books ·

An imprint of Penguin Group (USA) Inc.

DUTTON CHILDREN'S BOOKS

An imprint of Penguin Group (USA) Inc.

PUBLISHED BY THE PENGUIN GROUP

Penguin Group (USA) Inc., 375 Hudson Street, New York, New York 10014, U.S.A. • Penguin Group (Canada), 90 Eglinton Avenue East, Suite 700, Toronto, Ontario M4P 2Y3, Canada (a division of Pearson Penguin Canada Inc.) • Penguin Books Ltd, 80 Strand, London WC2R 0RL, England • Penguin Ireland, 25 St Stephen's Green, Dublin 2, Ireland (a division of Penguin Books Ltd) • Penguin Group (Australia), 250 Camberwell Road, Camberwell, Victoria 3124, Australia (a division of Pearson Australia Group Pty Ltd) • Penguin Books India Pvt Ltd, 11 Community Centre, Panchsheel Park, New Delhi—110 017, India • Penguin Group (NZ), 67 Apollo Drive, Rosedale, North Shore 0632, New Zealand (a division of Pearson New Zealand Ltd.) • Penguin Books (South Africa) (Pty) Ltd, 24 Sturdee Avenue, Rosebank, Johannesburg 2196, South Africa • Penguin Books Ltd, Registered Offices: 80 Strand, London WC2R 0RL, England

This book is a work of fiction. Names, characters, places, and incidents are either the product of the author's imagination or are used fictitiously, and any resemblance to actual persons, living or dead, business establishments, events, or locales is entirely coincidental.

The publisher does not have any control over and does not assume any responsibility for author or third-party websites or their content.

CIP Data is available.

Published in the United States by Dutton Children's Books,
an imprint of Penguin Group (USA) Inc.
345 Hudson Street, New York, New York 10014
www.penguin.com/youngreaders

Designed by Jason Henry
Printed in USA • First Edition
ISBN: 978-0-525-47691-7
1 3 5 7 9 10 8 6 4 2

To Quinn Rachel DeVillers

LYNNVISIBLE

That's certainly a bold fashion choice for your first day of high school," my mother said as I slid into a chair at our kitchen table.

"Ha-ha," I replied, tying my fuzzy bathrobe tighter around my pajamas. "Very funny. I decided I'd have breakfast *before* I got dressed."

"You only have half an hour before the bus comes," my mom warned as she stirred the mix for her traditional back-to-school pancakes. "You do know what you're wearing, right?"

"Mmmfh," I mumbled.

"I'll pretend that meant yes," my mom said, trying to get a splotch of pancake mix off her light blue button-down shirt. "Do you want chocolate chips in your pancakes?"

"That *is* a yes," I answered. That was an easy first-day-of-school decision. Unlike the other one: what to wear. I'd spent the last half hour standing paralyzed in my closet, unable to commit to the final outfit choice.

I mean, today was the day I'd be seeing my former middle-school classmates after a long summer. And seeing, for the first time, hundreds of new people from the other middle schools who were merging into one massive high school.

And *they'd* be seeing *me*. So, I needed the right outfit that would help me kick off my high school career and hopefully complete all my freshman year goals: being elected class president, being voted Homecoming Princess, going out with the quarterback, and getting straight A's.

HA. Just kidding.

My real goals were slightly less ambitious, though not necessarily easier for me to attain. I hoped to get through the year without a public humiliation and with somewhere to sit at lunch. Toss in a few decent grades and I'd consider my freshman year a rousing success.

The back door banged and I looked up to see my brother letting our dog inside. Bella came right over to me.

"You're so lucky, Bella. It's easy to get dressed when you're as cute as you. You look good in everything." I leaned over to scritch Bella under the collar of the pink-and-chocolate-brown striped sweater I had put on her that morning. She licked my hand and went off to her dog bowl.

My mom came over and put a plate of pancakes in front of me.

"Smells good," I said.

"Thanks," my brother responded, sliding into the chair across from me. "I used extra soap."

"Not you. Ew." I made a face. "I meant the pancakes. I don't even want to think about what you smell like."

"I smell good, and I look good," Dex said. He flexed his muscles. Or actually, muscle. Dex was not exactly a big guy. He was two years older than me, but an inch shorter. We shared the same scrawny, shrimpy build, but he was even shrimpier. His hair was light brown while mine was dark brown, but otherwise there was a definite resemblance in looks. In personality, not even.

"This is the Year of the Dex," my brother said. "Everyone's gonna want a piece of this."

I snorted.

"Snort all you want," Dex said, adjusting the collar of his blue-and-green plaid shirt. "Things are gonna be different this year, I can feel it. Maybe I will be Homecoming, Junior, *and* Senior Prom King."

"Maybe this is the year the Earth's orbit will shift and everyone will value your Geography Bee runner-up status," I said.

"I'll be champion this year; I can feel it," Dex said, pulling something out of his shirt pocket. "There's no stopping me now that I have my new phone complete with the latest, the greatest GPS. That's a Global Positioning System, Lynn. One press of the magic button and four satellites communicate and map exactly where I am at all times.

I can even see myself from three angles. Simultaneously."

I tuned him out. As would most of the people in our school, I had a feeling. I'm sure his GPS would be cool, I guess, if you were lost in the Himalayas, but Dex barely leaves his desktop computer.

"Right now I'm at 42.955 North and—"

"Sorry to break it to you," I cut him off, "but if you're reinventing yourself as Mr. Popularity, the cooler features of your cell phone are the video and fast Web access. Not the GPS."

"Well, then I can show them my homemade hydrogen fuel experiment on YouTube," Dex said. "I've got almost a thousand hits."

"The girls will be lining up," I muttered.

"Good attitude, Dex," my mom said, coming over to smooth Dex's hair. "Lynn, stop being so cynical. Why shouldn't your brother aim high in school? I think he'd make a wonderful Homecoming King."

"Is it disrespectful to call your mother delusional?" I asked. My mom threw her dish towel at my head.

"It's seven-o-two, time for the Year of the Dex to begin!" Dex said. He tossed his backpack on his back and grabbed car keys off the counter.

"Ahem," my mom said. "Those are *my* car keys."

"But, Ma!" Dex said. "You've been letting me use the car since I got my license!"

"*Share* my car," Mom said. "For the summer, Dex, and if you recall, we took turns with it. What do you think I'm going to do all day if you have my car?"

"You're working at home now," Dex said. "So, don't you stay at *home*?"

"Excuse me?" Mom said, giving him a look. She plucked the car keys from his hand. "Just because I'm no longer going to an office does not mean I do not need the car. Take the bus just like your sister."

"The bus?" Dex said. "This is so not cool."

"Then save up your own money for your own car," Mom said. "Today, these keys stay with me."

I felt a little sorry for Dex. It would seriously stink to ride the bus if you have your license. But I knew Mom would need the car. Ever since my dad moved across the country after they got divorced when I was ten, Mom had a lot to handle on her own. She recently started her own accounting business that she ran from our house.

"Fine," Dex grumbled. "But I'm not taking the bus. I'll ride my bike until I get *my own* car. Which will be soon."

Dex stomped out of the kitchen.

"Well, that wasn't the start-the-first-day-of-school-with-a-positive-attitude conversation I'd had in mind," my mom said. "May I start over with you, Lynn? May I give you a pep talk for your first day?"

"Sure," I said, taking a bite of pancake. "Go for it."

Mom started in on her "Smile at everyone, be friendly, and high school will be the best years of your life" speech.

I knew better. Just getting through middle school alive was a major deal for many of us. But now the stakes were even bigger. There were six middle schools all merging into one high school. In sum: new building, new teachers, new us. *Yipes.* I felt sick to my stomach. I pushed my pancakes away. I was too nervous to eat.

"I can't believe my little baby is starting high school," Mom continued. "It seems like just yesterday when you were born. I knew right away you were special. I said to myself, Lynn Vincent is destined to lead an interesting, exciting life!"

It was a good effort at a pep talk, but I highly doubted it. First off, she named me Lynn. Could there be a name any more boring and dull? Lynn is a middle name for people with cooler names like Angelina or Scarlett. Actually, Lynn's not even that cool for a middle name.

"So go out there and have a day to remember!" Mom was still going on and on. "Oh, speaking of remembering this day, I'm going to go grab my camera. I want to get a picture of you for my scrapbook. So don't leave yet."

Dex stuck his head back into the kitchen and looked hopefully at my mom.

"You, on the other hand, can leave," Mom said, and she went to get her camera. "I'm not changing my mind about the car."

"Man," Dex muttered under his breath as he left the kitchen. I heard the front door open and then—

Boom! Boom! Thud! AHHH!

I heard Dex yell. And a girl scream.

I jumped up and ran to the front door and saw Dex lying on the front lawn, holding his eye.

My best friend, Taylor, was standing on the front step.

"Omigosh, I'm so sorry," she was saying. "I was just going to ring the doorbell! I didn't mean to poke your eyeball, Dex! Or make you fall down the steps! I'm so sorry!"

"*Glar,*" Dex choked. He staggered away toward his bike.

"Have a good first day of school!" Taylor called after him. She turned to me. "Oops. And hi! Happy first day of school!"

"Not that I'm not glad to see you, but what are you doing here?" I asked her. Taylor lives as far away from me as you could and still go to the same middle school.

"I need you, Lynn," Taylor said. "I'm desperate."

That's when I noticed what Dex had tripped over. A backpack. And a tote bag. And a little suitcase. Taylor started to gather them up and drag them all into the house.

"Um, are you moving in?" I asked her.

"No, it's just, well—I had a First Day Fashion Panic Attack," Taylor said. She popped out the wheels on the suitcase and pulled it into the hall. "I was practically hyperventilating. So I brought a few things—okay, everything in my closet—with me so you could please, pretty please, help me figure out what to wear today."

"I thought you were all set," I said. "You've been planning for weeks."

"I know," Taylor said miserably. "I thought this outfit was perfect. But when I put my outfit on this morning, I realized something's not working."

I sighed. But I looked her up and down.

"It's the shoes, isn't it? These shoes don't look right, do they?" Taylor asked me.

Um. Not really.

"I knew it. I'll change my shoes," Taylor said. "Thanks for being honest."

And if she really wanted me to be honest, well, the shirt would have to go, too. And the pants were, well . . . The whole thing screamed Trying-Too-Hard-To-Be-Cool-While-Also-Being-Unflattering. So, if she was willing to let me do some damage control, I was itching to make some changes.

"Lynn! The bus is going to be here!" my mom called.

"Don't worry about that!" Taylor said brightly. "My mom is waiting outside to drive us to school."

I squinted. Her mother's SUV was parked down the street.

"She drove you over here for your first day outfit and now she's waiting for you?" I said.

"Actually she thinks we have a project together to take to school," Taylor admitted. "Which we do! Me! I made her park down there so your mom wouldn't see her and invite her in."

"You're crazy," I laughed. "But come on in and I'll help. I obviously have to get dressed, too."

"Thank you, you're saving my life," Taylor breathed, dragging her bags noisily across the brown hardwood.

"What is that noise?" My mom stepped in front of us. "Oh, hi, Taylor! Wonderful! You can be in the First Day of School Picture."

"Good morning, Mrs. Vincent!" Taylor said. "Lynn's going to help me pick something to wear today and give me a little fashion advice."

"Lynn is going to give you fashion advice?" My mom looked confused.

Okay, so my mom and I don't always agree about my style.

"Her mom's driving us to school," I assured my mom as we continued upstairs to my bedroom.

Taylor followed me into my room and waited as I put a Taylor-ish song on my iPod.

"So here's what I've got," Taylor said. She dumped her navy tote bag out on my white comforter. A stack of shirts fell out. She dumped last year's red backpack out. Jeans. Then she opened her suitcase and belts and shoes fell out.

"I brought extra earrings, too," Taylor said, digging through her purse.

"Wait, where are your books for school?" I asked her.

"In the car," Taylor said. "I ran out of room in the bags."

"First," I said, rifling through the piles of clothes, "we are, in magazine-speak, going to 'flatter your assets.'"

"Can you hide my big asset?" Taylor said hopefully. "Meaning my butt."

I ignored that.

"Try these." I tossed her a pair of jeans with what looked like the right angle of pockets. "If you wear this blue shirt—"

The blue shirt would bring out her blue eyes. I held up

a silvery tank that would look awesome with her skin tone and her blond hair she had flat-ironed to straightness.

Genius. And it would have looked *really* perfect with the shoes I knew would be hot soon but hadn't hit here yet. I'd bought them off eBay from someone in L.A. But they were too much of a statement for Taylor's personality, so I moved on. . . . Okay, these flats. So cute. Hmm, and the necklace that would pull it all together. Yup. Got it.

"You think?" Taylor said doubtfully as she took the shoes. "Those shoes aren't even new."

"Trust me," I said. "And use that tote bag for your book bag."

She took the clothes and went into my bathroom to get changed.

"How much do I hate my butt?" Taylor was moaning. "Why am I bothering to even try?"

"Just get dressed and come out here," I ordered. "And then look in the mirror."

She did. And when she saw herself, she smiled.

"Hey," Taylor said, "I kinda like this."

"Totally you," I agreed. "And that color brings out your tan."

"I do look tan for once." Taylor smiled. "Yay. And this outfit's even comfy. I was wondering how I was going to make it through the day in those other pants without breathing."

I watched her turn around in the mirror and smile at herself. And then she squealed.

"AHHH!!" she shrieked. "You shrank my butt! You are amazing and the best friend ever!!!" Taylor ran over and hugged me.

"No big deal," I told her, laughing. "Now get off me."

"It's a huge deal!" Taylor protested. "I owe you for life. Now, don't you need to get dressed?"

"Yup," I said. "Feel free to go have some of my mom's pancakes. I'll try to hurry."

Taylor went downstairs. And it was my turn.

Okay. This was crunch time. I needed inspiration. I turned on my iPod, scrolling through until I found the right song. Then I went into my closet, where I had the options all on hangers waiting for me to choose. It was a lot of pressure to make the right first impression. I thought of all the classmates I hadn't yet met thinking similar thoughts as they chose their first-day clothes. Trying to figure out exactly who they were, who they wanted to be, and to start off the year reflecting that and—I suddenly had a flash of fashion clarity.

I pulled the shirt from one outfit off its hanger. I matched it with the bottoms of another, and grabbed the shoes from a third. I mixed and matched and then—

Got it.

I put on my outfit and went into my bedroom to find Bella waiting for me.

"Hot or not, Bella?" I asked her, posing.

My dog cocked her head sideways to look.

"I think that was a yes?" I checked myself out in the

full-length mirror on the door of my closet. It looked right to me. I also turned around to check the back of my outfit while I was at it. I'd heard about the freshman who'd showed up on the first day with the back of her skirt tucked into her underwear; she'd walked around all day until a teacher finally broke it to her.

"Probably an urban legend, but you can't be too careful, right, Bella?" I asked my dog. "All right. I think I'm ready."

When I went downstairs, my mom was waiting with her camera.

"Doesn't Taylor look great?" I asked my mother.

"Yes, you certainly captured the beauty of the Taylor we know and love," Mom said. "And Lynn, you're absolutely sure of your outfit? You've made the final decision? First day of high school, first impressions?"

"Yup, Mom," I said firmly. "I'm good."

"Then stand together and say cheese," Mom said.

Taylor and I put our arms around each other and smiled as Mom took the picture.

"Let me see it." I took the camera from my mom and looked at the screen. There we were. Taylor smiling, in the outfit I'd put together, looking very happy.

And me, also looking very happy. In my navy-and-white plaid shirt. And my hot pink tutu skirt that flared out superwide. Belted with a wide black leather belt. I also wore my navy-and-white knitted kneesocks. On my head was a vintage black fedora with a large hot pink bow. And on my feet, sneakers that I'd hacked up and filled in the holes with tulle I'd trimmed off my skirt. And a necklace I'd made from old pink-and-red Polly Pocket shoes.

Yes, I know what you're thinking. *That's* what she's wearing the first day of school?

You won't be the only person thinking that today.

W e sat in the back row of Taylor's mom's SUV, pulling in to the drop-off line. First day of high school
is major. I mean, this is where I was going to be spending
the next four years of my life.

"Do I have anything in my teeth?" Taylor asked.

I checked. Nope.

"In my nose?"

"I'm *not* checking in your nose," I told her.

"Is my lip gloss too much? I feel smeary," she said.

"You're fine, you look great," I told her. "Really."

The car pulled up into the school parking lot. People
were getting off buses and out of their cars. And there was
my brother on his bike. Poor Dex. I felt sorry for him for
a half second until I saw him looking up and then at his
phone, mapping his GPS location.

"I think I'm going to puke," Taylor said.

"That's one way to get noticed," I said.

Taylor looked at me. I knew what she was thinking. We'd get noticed no matter what. And it wasn't because of her.

"You know your life would be so much easier if you'd wear something like this, too," Taylor said carefully.

I know. Yes, it would have been much easier for me to put on the typical high-schooler outfit. A cute hoodie with a little skirt or a pair of jeans and I would fit right in. Spend my whole high school career under the radar, nobody noticing me.

"Part of me wishes I could." I sighed. "But face it, I just have to be me, even if I'm labeled Freak Girl. My outfit represents the trauma girls face getting ready for the first day of school. It asks 'Do I have to be put into a category on the first day of school?' So the navy-and-white plaid represents the traditional school uniform, while the hot pink tutu skirt is the total opposite. The bow is girly, the sneakers sporty, the leather is tough. The hat is retro, the socks crafty. Answering 'No, I don't fit any category.'"

"I get it," Taylor said. "Like how I couldn't figure out what to wear today."

That's why I love her.

"And the Polly Pocket necklace?" Taylor asked.

"A nod to the simpler days of childhood," I said. "Before all the drama and crazy began. But seriously, now's your chance to dissociate from me and start fresh. You can ask your mom to drop you off separately so you aren't seen with me as you walk in. I'm okay with it."

Just then Mrs. Snyder called to us.

"Lynn, would it be easier for me to drop you off here, since, *ahem*, your homeroom is at this end of the school? I can take Taylor closer to hers?"

Taylor's mom was obviously thinking the same thing. Taylor's mom didn't want her to be seen with me—today or pretty much any day I knew. Taylor's mom had encouraged her to have more "traditional friends" ever since we'd met.

I'd met Taylor in sixth grade. Our elementary schools had fed into the same middle school. I met Taylor by accident. I'd walked into the cafeteria and started to scope out where to sit.

I still think my outfit that day was cute. A purple Hello Kitty shirt I'd shredded and layered over a white tee. An electric blue bubble-hem swing skirt, a yellow belt, and jelly shoes. I wore dangly yellow smiley-face earrings. (Okay, in hindsight, the large bow I'd worn on my head was a fashion oops. I thought it perfectly represented the happy freedom of middle school, where we would change classes and have our own lockers.)

But when I walked into the lunchroom I got my usual looks. Like, *WHAT is that girl wearing?!*

So I'd stood there in the cafeteria, and this girl came up to me. She had curly blond hair and was wearing a light pink T-shirt that said I ❤ KITTENS with baggy khaki pants.

"Hi, it's me, Taylor!" she said cheerfully. "We're sitting over here."

"Um, okay," I said. Had I missed something? I had no

idea who Taylor was. But she was waving me to follow her, so I went and sat down. There were three other girls sitting with her.

"We're all here now!" Taylor said to all of us. "First, I want to say *Bun venit*! That means 'Welcome' in Romanian! I'll introduce everyone. Caroline, Lucy, and Camille."

Everyone was like, Hi!

"How do you like school so far?" Taylor asked me.

"Um, pretty good," I said. "I found all my classes at least."

"Wow, you speak really good English," the girl named Lucy said.

"She's right! You don't even have an accent," Taylor said.

"Huh? Me? Why would I have an accent?" I asked.

Everyone looked at me. I looked back at them, confused. "Didn't you just move here a couple weeks ago?" Taylor asked. "From Romania?"

Um, no. I shook my head.

"Omigosh! Omigosh, omigosh. I'm so sorry!" Taylor said. "I thought you were Dominique, the new student from Romania!"

Everyone was silent.

Oh. I got it. Because of my clothes.

"See, I'm the New Student Guide and this is the New Student Table and—" Taylor kept going. Her face turned bright red.

"Sorry for the misunderstanding," I said, picking up my

lunch things. I noticed a confused-looking girl still wandering around the cafeteria. "That might be Dominique, over there."

"Omigosh!" Taylor said. Then she turned to me. "You sit right there, 'kay? I'll be right back!"

I sat down at the table. Well, at this point, the lunchroom was in full force. I didn't want to stand up and try to find a new table. We all watched as Taylor went over and talked to the confused girl. Taylor brought the girl back to our table.

"Everybody! *This* is Dominique," Taylor said brightly. "Let's welcome her to the New Student Table!"

"Bun venit!" I said to Dominique.

Taylor sat down next to me and spent the whole lunch period apologizing for the screwup. Taylor ended up in my math class, too, and got in trouble for talking—because she was still whispering apologies to me.

So that's how we met. Dominique joined the soccer team and left to sit with them at lunch. Caroline moved to the Popular Table. Lucy and Camille went to the Drama People Table. But somehow, I stayed at the New Student Table with Taylor. And we've pretty much been there ever since. I guess we shouldn't really call it the New Student Table anymore. Mostly, it's just us.

Taylor's mom wishes she'd move from the New Student Table to the Popular Table. And also from me. Especially now, I can tell, on our first day of high school. Taylor's mom kind of intimidates me. I feel like any moment she might ground Taylor from me or something, so I lay low around her.

"I hate when my mom does this," Taylor whispered. Then she raised her voice. "Doesn't Lynn look cool, Mom?"

I gave her a look. She wasn't helping me lay low.

"Lynn is certainly . . . visible," her mother said.

"What, do you want her to be *invisible*?" Taylor asked.

"Yes, she does," I whispered, and elbowed Taylor. "She wants me invisible. I'm going to get out first like your mother said. You can go in, making your own impression without me."

It wasn't like her mother was wrong. I'm sure people would be looking at me. Only one-sixth of the people here were used to me. That meant five-sixths would see me for the first time. But just because I chose to torture myself didn't mean Taylor had to suffer.

"Don't be silly," Taylor said. "Ignore my mother. You're my best friend and of course I'll be seen with you—oh no! *Duck!*"

Taylor ducked her head. Then she grabbed me and pulled me down with her until we were scrunched down on the floor of the car together.

"That didn't last long," I said. "Changed your mind about not being seen with me?"

"It's not that!" Taylor said, sounding slightly panicky.

"Then why are we hiding?" I asked.

Mrs. Snyder sang out: "Oh, look, Taylor! It's Chasey!"

"Just keep going, Ma." Taylor hissed. She lowered her voice, almost talking to herself. "I don't want to start off high school with a Chasey Welch experience."

Too late.

"Yoo-hoo!" Taylor's mother was rolling down her window and calling out, "Yoo-hoo! Chasey!"

I peeked out the window. I saw Chasey and her crew getting out of a black convertible. Chasey. Platinum hair, stick straight. She was also as skinny as a stick. She was totally on trend in her exactly-what-the-freshman-IT-Girl-should-wear-on-the-first-day outfit. Zero points for originality, though, since I'd seen the entire outfit in one of the magazines, including the shoes. But one hundred points for being able to afford it . . . and look good in it.

I hoped Chasey didn't hear Mrs. Snyder or would just ignore her, like she ignored most everyone outside her inner circle. Chasey and I had been in elementary school together. She's the kind of girl that the teachers love because she acts so sweet and charming. The parents love her because she acts so sweet and charming. It's just an act. She's not sweet or charming.

Taylor had gone to a different elementary school, but she knew Chasey because their families belonged to the same country club. They used to swim together in the summer with the same group. Then, the summer before middle school, Taylor was disinvited.

"It was the first day the pool opened," Taylor had told me. "I went over to the deck chairs where we always sat. Everyone threw their towels over the empty chairs. And

Chasey goes, "Sorry, Taylor, this is now a loser-free zone. Maybe you can find some friends at the baby pool."

"Yoo-hoo! Chasey!" Mrs. Snyder was not giving up.

"Hello, Mrs. Snyder." Chasey waggled her fingers. And kept walking with her friends.

"Keep driving, Ma!" Taylor was practically begging.

But Mrs. Snyder was on a mission. The car slowed, then stopped. The horn beeped. And then Chasey's face was leaning in the front window.

"Good morning, Mrs. Snyder," Chasey said sweetly.

"Chasey, you look so lovely and grown up," Mrs. Snyder said. "How's your mother? I've been meaning to call her about the mother-daughter tea at the club."

"Oh, great," Taylor groaned in my ear.

"Taylor, say hello to Chasey," Mrs. Snyder asked. "Taylor, where are you?"

"I think she's on the floor of your backseat?" Chasey giggled. "Happy first day of high school, Taylor!"

Taylor turned red. She sat up slowly.

"Hi, Chasey," Taylor grumbled.

"And is that Liz on the floor next to you?" Chasey leaned in farther and smirked.

Please. She knows my name.

"Why don't I drop you girls off and you can all walk with Chasey into school for your first day?" Mrs. Snyder said.

For a second, Chasey was at a loss for words. Then she recovered.

"I'd love to, but I have to meet with the, uh, social committee," Chasey said, pointing at her groupies. "We're planning the, uh, social! Buh-bye!"

"Tell your mother I said hello!" Mrs. Snyder sang out to Chasey's retreating back.

"She is such a sweet girl. Taylor, that sounds like a perfect activity for you to join," Mrs. Snyder said. "The social committee with Chasey!"

"Antisocial committee, maybe," Taylor muttered under her breath. I noticed her cheeks were bright pink, and she was chewing on her hair.

"You okay?" I said to Taylor.

She nodded, but she didn't meet my eyes as the car started back up again.

"Have a fabulous first day of school!" Mrs. Snyder said. "Wait, Taylor, don't get out yet. Push your bangs back. There, much better."

Taylor took a deep breath and opened the car door. I followed her out of the car.

"Thanks, Mrs. Snyder," I said.

"Taylor! Your pants cuff is slightly crooked! Fix your pants!" I heard Mrs. Snyder call out.

"She's so embarrassing," Taylor said, reaching down to adjust her pants. "Everyone is staring at me."

Not exactly. Oh, they *were* staring in our direction, but they were staring at me. I held my head high and kept walking. I saw some people turn and look at me. *Yes, yes, I know. My outfit is unique. I know. I'm expressing myself, thank you.* I lifted my chin higher.

"Hi, Karly! Hi, Melissa!" Taylor called out. They waved to us.

"Hi, Lauren! Hi, Alicia!" Those girls didn't wave back.

"Check out the freak!" Another girl walked by with her friends and pointed at me.

Thank you for the nice welcome to high school. I told myself that everyone was nervous. Some people chose to express their nervousness in immature ways, say, by calling another classmate a freak. I wouldn't stoop to that level. We're in high school now, people.

I kept my smile on and ignored them. I was fully aware that my style was not for everyone. But I was hopeful that somewhere in this school, there would be some people who might appreciate fashion creativity and expression. And suddenly the bell rang and there was an insane crowd of bodies squishing past each other to get to their lockers.

"See you at lunch!" Taylor yelled to me, and then it seemed like she was swept off in the crowd.

I pushed through the crowd and looked at the locker numbers until I got to mine. Unfortunately there was someone in front of it. Or make that two someones, attached at the lips.

I cleared my throat. Makeout Couple continued.

"Excuse me," I said. *"Excuse me."*

They came up for air only to slide down a few lockers. Then they continued their smoochfest. I tried not to look and focused on my locker combination.

19-24-16.

I yanked at it. Nothing.

19-24-16.

Still nothing.

"Oh, come on, locker!" I muttered. The girl half of Makeout Couple looked over at me. Oh great, she's probably thinking, *Not only does that girl dress weird but she talks to herself.*

I kicked my locker with my shoe.

My shoe was really cute, I had to say. I held my foot out and admired it. I'd done a good job decorating the sides. *I think I will do another pair in silver and yellow, and maybe some polka dots and*—the bell rang again. This was probably not the time for my shoe. *Focus, Lynn, focus. 19-24-16 . . .*

I heard a click and Yeeess! The lock popped open! I flung the locker open in victory! And—

"OW!"

Oh! The locker door had swung open and hit the person at the next locker.

"Oops, sorry!" I said. I pulled my locker closed.

I looked at the guy rubbing his head.

His head was full of curly dark brown hair. Shiny, curly, dark brown hair.

"I'm really sorry," I said.

"It's okay." The guy looked up at me. "I'm fine."

And yes, he *was* fine.

Very fine. I sneaked a glance at him while he got some books from his locker. He was wearing a basic charcoal gray tee and jeans. And then I saw them. He was wearing dark green sneakers. Not just any sneakers—vintage, retro, very cool.

That did it. I was in love. At least with his sneakers. I looked up at the guy, still rubbing his head. I should say something. More apologies? Introduce myself? Hi, I'm Lynn. Hi, I'm Lynn.

And then some girls walking by started laughing.

"Did you see that? *So* weird!" one of the girls said, turning to look back at me.

I slammed my locker shut and took off before the guy could see my face turning as pink and red as my Polly Pocket shoe necklace.

After the last bell, I hurried up to my locker. Of course, my last class was totally on the other side of the school, so I had to hurry up or I'd miss my bus. When I walked down the hall, I was happy to see Taylor, standing near my locker. I wasn't as happy to see the Makeout Couple going at it, directly in front of my locker.

"Hey!" I said, going up to Taylor. "I'm dying to hear about your day but I have to catch my bus."

"No worries!" Taylor said. "My mom said she'd drive us home!"

"Really?" I said. Awesome. I hated the bus.

"I was going to wait at your locker, but . . ." Taylor tilted her head.

"Yeah. Makeout Couple was there earlier, too," I said.

I went up to them and cleared my throat.

"Excuse me," I said. "I need to get to my locker."

They barely unlocked lips as they moved down the row.

"Awkward," I said as I worked my lock.

"I think it's romantic," Taylor said. "They don't even want to be separated. Maybe someday I'll meet my Mr. Romance. Maybe even . . . today!"

"You met someone already?" I looked at her. "Did you have some love connection in class?"

"I wish," Taylor said. "I didn't talk to one single guy today, besides my science teacher. But the day is not over!"

"Um, it kind of is," I said. "Unless your mom is driving some cute guys, too?"

"No, just you and me," Taylor said cheerfully. "She said she can pick us up later. So, we just have to kill a little time first."

She was up to something. I gave her a look.

"What?" Taylor said innocently. "We can wait for my mom at, say, FonDo."

We can? FonDo was the afterschool hangout place. It was kind of a see-and-be-seen place. Not my thing. I'd been *seen* enough today.

"I'll pass," I said. "You know I'm not a FonDo kind of person."

"Um," Taylor said. "We kind of have to go to FonDo. One of my mom's friends told her it was the cool place to go, so she told me she'd pick us up there."

"Maybe it's not too late for me to catch the bus," I grumbled.

"Well," Taylor kept talking, "the good news is this girl I met in band said she could go over early and snag us a table."

"Then you don't need me if you have someone else," I said.

"I *always* need you. And really, it could be fun. We can celebrate our first day. Pretty please? I'll be your best friend?"

Taylor wouldn't stop begging until I'd agreed. So we walked over to FonDo.

I had to admit the place was sweet. There were soft squishy couches to sit on and a fireplace in the middle. The walls were pale green and cream with cocoa accents. I immediately thought of this pale green sweater I had that was begging to be deconstructed. If I added some cream lace to it, some cocoa accents around the sleeves . . .

"Lynn!" Taylor said. "Earth to Lynn!"

"Sorry!" I said. "I spaced out."

"There's Grace from band," Taylor said, making her way to a booth near the front where a girl was working on a laptop. Grace had straight black hair. She was wearing a putty-colored shirt, long white shorts, and mushroom-colored flip-flops.

Taylor slid into the booth across from Grace.

"Grace, this is Lynn," Taylor said.

"Hi," I said, careful not to slide into the booth until I gauged the reaction.

I saw Grace's eyes get wide for a second. Then she smiled.

"It's nice to meet you," Grace said.

"This is an awesome booth," I said, sitting down next to her. It was right in the middle of everything.

"My cousin's a senior," Grace explained, pointing to a girl at another booth. "She gets to leave early, so she saved this for us."

"How cool is that?" Taylor said. "Is anyone else coming?"

"No, you're pretty much the only person who talked to me today," Grace said. "I went to this private school across town, so I don't know anyone here."

"I didn't even know she was new!" Taylor said to me. "It's like I have radar from my New Student Table."

Taylor started telling Grace about her New Student Table at middle school. I opened the menu and read about all the things you could dip into chocolate or cheese fondue.

"This is the way coolest hangout!" Taylor was looking around enthusiastically. "I heard everyone who's anyone in high school comes here. Yummy food, comfy couches . . . and Lynn, isn't that Dex?"

I looked up. My Dex was walking down the aisle. Oh, ugh. My brother was going to be hanging out at FonDo, too? And he was walking directly toward us. Wait, he wasn't going to try to sit with us, was he?

Then I saw the little badge.

FonDo it with . . . DEX

FonDo it with Dex? My brother was working at FonDo? 'Kay, *greeaaat*.

"Welcome to FonDo," he said. "I'm Dex, and I'll be

here to help you today. Are you sure you girls are old enough to be here without your moms?"

"We're high schoolers!" Grace said nervously. "My cousin's a senior and—"

"It's okay, Grace," I said. "That's my brother. He's being obnoxious, as usual."

"Hi, Dex!" Taylor said. "Looks like most of the swelling went down!"

Dex touched his eye.

"Taylor knocked him down our steps today," I explained to Grace.

"I'll just stand over here," Dex said, moving away from Taylor. "That way no one gets injured."

"Okay, so when did you start working here?" I asked Dex.

"About"—Dex looked at his watch—"two hours ago. Some guy quit today, so they called me in. Excellent, huh? I'm going to make some money for my convertible."

"You have a convertible?" Grace asked.

"Well, not exactly," Dex said. "But when I'm done with my shift, I'll have twenty-two dollars saved up. Plus tips. So let's get a move on, people. The more tables I wait on, the more moola I make. What do you want?"

"How about the FonDo Fabulous Fiesta?" Taylor read from the menu. "'Milk chocolate swirled with cookie crumbs, perfect for celebrations.'"

"It comes with fruit, marshmallows, and cheesecake pieces for dipping," Dex recited.

"Perfect," Taylor said happily. "Dex, it's so cool you're

working here. You're going to get a front row seat to everything high school—the hookups and breakups and make-ups! Any good drama yet?"

"Uh, table five thought their fondue wasn't hot enough and wanted to complain to the manager," Dex said.

"Keep your eyes and ears peeled, Dex," Taylor told him. "We're right in the middle of the action. Look, there's Kameela 'the Boyfriend Stealer' Jones over there with Will 'Will he please take off his shirt and show me his eight-pack' Liu! And look who's walking in now—Arin Morgan!"

That got Dex's attention. He turned around to look.

This girl with long, supermodel-shiny mahogany hair had just come through the door. She had the Achingly-Perfect-and-It-Comes-Effortlessly-for-Me look.

We weren't the only ones watching her as she walked in the door.

"Arin Morgan is a senior," Taylor explained. "*The* senior. They might as well cancel all voting this year, because she'll definitely be Homecoming Queen and Prom Queen."

Arin was stopping at booths and saying hi and hugging people all over the place. She stopped at a booth where everyone was like, Hiiii! Hiiiii!

"Arin Morgan owns this world," Taylor sighed. "The rest of us just live in it."

My brother was still watching Arin wave and hug as he picked up the napkins.

"Stop drooling," I told my brother. "She is so out of your league."

"Maybe she likes a man in a uniform," Dex said. He pulled up his shirtsleeve, flexed his muscles, and posed. We all started cracking up.

Then I noticed Arin Morgan heading our way.

"Uh, Dex!" I said. "Heads up."

Dex turned around. He stopped mid-pose and froze when he saw Arin walk by our booth.

"Now *that's* good customer service," Arin said to him.

Dex turned bright red as Arin smiled and walked to the booth behind ours.

"I'll go get your spoons," he croaked, and fled.

"So she's perfect *and* nice?" Grace said.

"Oh, please. She's probably one of those girls who smiles at everyone to their face," Taylor said glumly. "And then they're totally nasty behind your back."

"Shh," I warned. "She *is* behind us."

I heard people saying hi to her as Arin slid into the booth of people directly behind us. Okay. The back of Arin's head was right behind me. We probably looked like a before and after hair commercial.

We all got all silent at our table. I think we all didn't want to say anything stupid. Like the popular people were actually going to listen to us. Or even be aware of our existence. But still.

Awkward. Then I heard Dex's voice behind us.

"Uh, hey, I'm Dex," I could hear him say. "How would you like to do it with FonDo?"

I heard giggles.

"Dex is waiting on Arin's table and I hear laughing," I said. "Oh no. Taylor, you have the best view—are they laughing at him or with him?"

"With him, I think," Taylor reported. "Yup, he's smiling."

"Really?" I said. I turned to Grace to explain. "My brother is somewhat awkward around girls."

"I'm telling you, that is the magic of this place," Taylor said. "I mean, look at *us*. We're here at a prime table, rubbing shoulders with the rich and glamorous of Independence High School. See, Lynn? I told you we should come."

I had to agree; this was all going pretty well. I'd possibly made a new friend, I had an inside connection at FonDo, even if it was just Dex. I was feeling, well, like I kind of belonged here, like I fit in.

"Oh my gaw, look at that girl's outfit," some girl snorted as she walked by our booth.

Or . . . maybe not.

Grace shrunk in her seat and looked uncomfortable. It dawned on me that she might not be up for getting negative attention for being seen in public with me.

"Um, I need to go to the girls' room," I said, standing up.

"I'll go with her," Taylor said to Grace. "We'll be right back."

I walked quickly to the bathroom without looking at anyone. I went in and looked under the stalls for feet. The coast was clear.

"You okay?" Taylor asked me.

"You know what, I'm going to wait outside," I said. "You and Grace can hang here; really, it's fine. I told you this wasn't exactly my scene."

I'd been having a happy moment, and then those girls started with the whole laughing at me. I've been teased way worse, of course. Teased, ignored, had people make faces at me, since as far back as I could remember. In preschool, people would say how cute I was when I showed up in my Tinkerbell costume. But by kindergarten, I was the only girl who still wore her Tinkerbell costume in public. I think the eye rolling started then.

In first grade, I wore a tutu over my pants to school because I was excited about starting ballet class. Why I wore this with rain boots, I can't remember. But I remember this boy in my class asked if I thought it was Halloween.

In third grade, I learned to sew. I made a skirt out of two school T-shirts to show school spirit and proudly wore it to school. In hindsight, the pom-poms I'd attached to the bottom were probably overkill, not to mention difficult to move in. The girls moved away from me at the lunch table.

In fifth grade, I was upset about endangered owls, so I made myself a brown outfit with a little owl on it reflecting my desire to help save them. I now agree with the girls who laughed, saying that the jacket I'd made of fake feathers made me look more like a chicken, but I still think it was for a good cause.

I could go on and on. You'd think I'd be way used to it now. It's just . . .

"I thought people in high school would be more . . . accepting," I told Taylor. "Or there'd be someone at least a little like me? Where are my people?"

"Uh, I'm your people," Taylor said.

"I didn't meant that," I told her. "Sorry, I just meant I'm tired of getting stomped on just because, you know, I express myself through my clothes."

"You're right! I'm tired of it for you!" Taylor said. "No more getting stomped on! No more getting stepped on or trompled on!"

"I'm not sure *trompled* is even a word," I said.

"Whatever," Taylor said. "We're not getting trompled on anymore! Come on!"

Taylor flung the bathroom door open and marched out, leaving me with not much choice but to follow her. I followed her back to our booth, not looking to see if people were looking at me. I kept my head high, my eyes straight forward, and I slid into our booth seat next to Grace.

Except it wasn't Grace. It was . . . huh? Chasey Welch? And some people I didn't know, and huh?

"Um, sorry, I'm in the wrong seat," I stammered. I looked at Taylor, who was standing there, looking slightly frozen. I turned around and saw Arin and her friends sitting in the booth behind ours. Wait, this *was* our booth.

"I think this is our booth," I said to Chasey.

"I'm blanking on your name," Chasey said. "Um, Liz, right?"

"Yeah, it's Liz," I said. "That's it."

"Your friend switched tables. I think she's waiting for

you over there," Chasey said, pointing toward the back. I squinted. I could just barely see Grace sitting at a table back by the bathrooms.

"So buh-bye," Chasey said.

Um, huh?

"Liz, you're too visible up here," Chasey said patronizingly as she looked me slowly up and down. "Your table's back there."

I opened my mouth to stand up to her, but nothing came out.

"Come on, Lynn," Taylor said quietly, and started walking to the back. I followed her, hearing laughter behind me.

"What just happened?" I asked Grace after Taylor and I had sat down in the chairs at the new table.

"Your friend came over and said you and Taylor wanted to give her your table," Grace said. "The blond girl? She said you guys wanted to sit here instead?"

Taylor and I looked at each other.

"Chasey stole our booth," I said.

"We've been trompled," Taylor sighed.

"I'm sorry," Grace said. "She was pretty convincing."

"Oh, she's convincing, all right," Taylor said glumly. "You didn't stand a chance."

"Why would she steal our booth?" Grace asked.

Hmm. Let's see. Our booth had been:

1. In the center of everything, so she can see and be seen?

· 38 ·

2. Conveniently located next to Arin's IT table?

3. Occupied by people you think will just get up and move because you and your clones say so?

Swell. I slumped into an empty seat.

"This table is just as good, don't you think?" Taylor said brightly. Then the toilet in the girls' room flushed. Loudly.

"Look on the bright side—if we have to go to the bathroom, look how convenient this is!" Taylor added.

"Nice try," I said. I should have seen this coming. I thought about how Chasey had said, "Lynn you're too visible." Well, yes, I knew I was visible in the clothes I chose to wear. But why did everything have to suddenly seem so . . . humiliating?

"Oh great, now Chasey is stealing our food, too?" Taylor grumped.

Dex had brought a tray over to our ex-booth. I saw Chasey say something to him and point to the back. Dex walked through the aisle toward us.

"Are you okay now, Taylor?" Dex said, setting the tray down on our table.

"Is she okay about what?" I asked him.

"Lynn, that's not cool to call attention to Taylor's problem," Dex said. "It's gotta be embarrassing enough."

"What embarrassing problem?" Taylor asked.

"The uh, bladder thing?" Dex said. "Your friend at your old booth said you had to change tables so Taylor could be near the bathroom so she could pee all the time."

"Okay, that is so uncool," I said. "Taylor doesn't have a bladder problem. We, however, have a Chasey problem."

"Oh." Dex shrugged. "Well, you said there was lots of drama at FonDo, so here's your catfight. Bring on the popcorn!"

"Aren't you supposed to stick up for your own sister?" I asked him.

"Oh, yeah, I guess," Dex said. "Want me to spit in her nonfat vanilla latte no whipped cream?"

"Okay, ew, no," I said. "Well, I kinda do, but that's not a good idea."

"Well, enjoy your food," Dex said. "One FonDo Fiesta."

"Yum," Taylor said. "At least it will help cheer us up."

We each took a long fork. I stabbed a piece of cake and dipped it in the bowl of melted chocolate.

"So are *you* okay?" Grace looked at me.

"About what?" I tried to feign ignorance about what she was talking about.

"About what that girl said before you left the table," she clarified. "Seriously, I don't understand why people think they can be so rude."

"I'm kinda used to it," I said. "I guess I bring it on myself because I like to dress this way."

"I bet Gwen Stefani was once like you," said Grace.

"I appreciate the thought," I said. "Too bad I can't sing or dance and have no talent."

"You have talent," Taylor protested. "Just not talent that's always appreciated around here."

"May I ask what you're supposed to be?" Grace asked. "You're not goth, you're not emo, you're not preppy . . ."

"Um, I'm not really supposed to *be* anything. Just . . . unique. Individual," I said. "Just expressing myself through what I'm wearing. I dunno, I'm just being . . . me."

"I'm obviously not into fashion," Grace said, pointing at her outfit. "But I guess I express myself when I'm playing flute or piano."

"I don't express myself through anything," Taylor said. "That makes me what? Unexpressed? Repressed? Depressed?"

"You play flute, too," Grace said. "Don't you feel like playing music expresses a deep inner part of yourself?"

"Erm, no," Taylor said. "I take flute because in middle school you had to pick band or choir, and my voice is excruciating. But, Lynn, Grace is really good at flute. She's first chair. I'm about nine hundred and ninety-ninth."

"You're not nine hundred and ninety-ninth," Grace scolded her. "And you sounded good, by the way. I could hear you behind me."

"Not compared to you," Taylor insisted. "Your solo was amazing."

"Thanks." Grace smiled. "I can show you something my flute teacher just taught me." She pulled a flute out of a black flute case and they talked flute, as I half spaced out.

I dipped a marshmallow in the chocolate and watched a girl with red hair come out of the bathroom. Ooh, I really liked that girl's shirt. I turned around to see what the back looked like. It would look very cool if I ripped out the neckline and—

I felt a kick under the table.

"Lynn," Taylor whispered. "Don't be so obvious. Don't give Chasey the satisfaction of staring at her."

"I'm not looking at Chasey," I insisted.

"Oh, ugh, look, Chasey's all over that guy!" Taylor said, craning her neck. "Figures, he's hot, too."

"Don't we have better things to talk about besides Chasey?" I said. "Seriously. Turn around and stop looking at them—hey, she totally is sitting on his lap. She's practically wrapped around him."

"See?" Taylor said. "Even you're watching her now."

"Am not," I lied. But I was. More people had joined them, sitting on the back of the booth. Our old booth was now the center of the freshman universe.

Taylor's cell phone went off.

"It's my mother," Taylor groaned. She opened it up. "Hello? But you said four thirty . . . No. NO! NO! We'll meet you outside."

Taylor hung up the phone and dropped her half-eaten marshmallow.

"Uh-oh," she said. "Lynn and I have to get out of here. And fast. If we don't meet my mother outside, you just know she'll come in and humiliate us."

Taylor's mother? In here? Nothing good could come of that. I started waving down my brother. Waiter! Waiter!

"It's fine, I understand," Grace said. "My mom will be here any minute to take me to piano lessons, anyway."

Dex came over to us. "Leaving so soon? Don't forget my well-deserved tip."

"Taylor's mom is giving me a ride home," I said. "Can you hurry up with the bill? It's an emergency."

"I do have other customers," Dex said. "Potential big tippers."

"Just take this," I pleaded, giving him a hard-earned twenty-dollar bill from babysitting. "Keep the change! And you can eat our leftovers!"

"It was my pleasure to serve you," Dex said, pocketing the money.

I turned to Grace. "It was really cool to meet you. I hope we can do this again."

Taylor was quickly packing up her backpack when I saw the white SUV pull up out front.

"Taylor! Your mom's here!" I said, and turned. I managed to knock over her small plate with the gooey marshmallow still on it. It dripped down the table and then on to Grace's flute case.

"I'm so sorry," I told her, looking at the mess. "Let me clean that off."

"I got it, don't worry," Grace said. "Really, go."

"Hurry!" Taylor urged me.

I followed her but then looked down. Oh great, I had marshmallow goo on my knit socks. I tried to scrape it off, but it was too sticky. I quickly walked out behind Taylor. I didn't look at anyone while I was walking out. Especially at Chasey's booth. Walking, walking. Except then . . . I stopped.

Not on purpose. I mean, I tried to keep walking. But something tugged on my leg . . . I looked down. Oh no. One of my socks was unraveling where the marshmallow goo had stuck. The yarn was caught on something—OMG. It was wrapped around a chair.

Alrighty. So there I was, standing right in front of Chasey and everyone in her booth. And I'm stuck.

"Helloo? May we help you?" Chasey leaned over to ask.

"Um, no, thanks," I said. I tried to subtly untangle the yarn without being obvious, but it wasn't happening.

"Ha, she's stuck," one of the girls said.

I tried to be casual as I watched some of them lean over to see what she was talking about. I froze a smile on my face. *Go back to your conversation! Nothing to see here!* I bent down and tried to untangle the yarn. I saw Taylor outside the door waving at me, like, What are you doing?

"Dude, check it out, her clothes are coming off," one of the guys said, laughing. "Woo hoo! Take it *all* off, baby!"

They all started cracking up. I could feel my face turn bright red. I just wanted out of there. My sock was not untangling. I'd have to sacrifice my sock, along with my pride. I started to yank harder. I closed my eyes and tugged.

"Here, let me help."

I opened my eyes. This guy slid out of the booth and bent down to help me. I noticed the green vintage shoes. Oh! It was the guy from the locker next to me.

"Wait," he said. "If you just pull it, you'll ruin it."

"It doesn't matter," I said. I felt that deep hot embarrassment seeping through me. I just wanted to get out of there before I died of it.

"Naw, I can save it, I think," he said. "There, I got it!"

The yarn was unstuck. He handed me the unraveled yarn. Tangled, but not broken.

"You did it!" I said. "Um, thanks."

I got that feeling in my stomach. He was seriously cute when he smiled at me.

"No prob," he said. "See you at the locker tomorrow."

I couldn't help smiling. He recognized me. He noticed me. (Well, duh. I'm hard not to notice.) He stood there looking at me and smiling. I was smiling back. It was like a moment straight out of a movie!!!

"Okay, bye," I stammered. I shoved my backpack on my back and started walking toward the door.

"Those Marc Jacobs kneesocks were kinda cute," I heard a girl in the booth say.

"Oh, puh-lease," Chasey said. "You're kidding, right? That girl makes her own clothes. She's a total freak."

Okay, maybe the movie was *Mean Girls*.

I clutched my yarn and limped out the door.

Two ties, one twist and there. Almost good as new. You almost couldn't tell where the sock had unraveled. I held it and admired my work.

"Almost as good as new, Bella," I said.

Bella rolled over on her side and scratched at her black lace tank top.

"Too itchy?" I asked her, and took the shirt off her as she sighed in relief. "Pugs shouldn't suffer for fashion."

I shouldn't have to either. I shoved the socks into one of my drawers. I didn't know if I could bring myself to wear them again. If I was going to pull off my unique style, it would certainly help if I didn't get stuck and then unravel in front of people.

I needed to think about something else. I'd go to my closet to escape. My closet always, always made me feel better.

When we'd moved to this house, my mom was surprised I didn't lobby for the bigger bedroom. But I totally wanted this one, the small room . . . with the walk-in closet.

I picked up Bella and pushed through the black-and-white beads I'd strung and hung across my closet like a curtain.

Ahhhhh . . . My walk-in closet. The one place in the world that was totally me.

It was like my own world. I turned on my iPod and set it to my Fashion Inspiration Playlist and took a moment to soak everything in. I had painted the inside of my closet a perfect shade of robin's egg blue. Along the top I'd painted words that inspired me: CONFIDENCE * CREATIVITY * SELF-EXPRESSION * REACTION *

I had white hooks where I could piece together outfits and hang them up. Another outfit could hang on the black dress form that stood off to the side.

One of the walls was filled with shelves full of fabrics and materials. Velvet, shiny, bright, muted. Everything was ripe to become shirts or bags or who knows what. I spent all of my babysitting money, my birthday money, my small allowance on this stuff, but it was completely worth it to me.

The last wall was my inspiration board. I tacked up pictures of anything that inspired me in one giant collage, reaching almost to the ceiling. I had my favorite story-boards, which were sketches of designs in colored pencils. Some had swatches of fabric stapled to the page to add texture and color.

It was the wall that inspired me whenever I was getting

dressed or making a creation. My Wall of LynnSpiration. Across the top of the collage I'd written the name of my pretend store: LYVIN. It was my name mixed together, LynnVincent, and I'd always thought it could stand for Lynn Vintage, too. Like, my clothes would someday, in the future, be valued and appreciated. They certainly weren't now, at least by my peers. But whatever.

I put Bella down in the furry zebra-print chair, and she sighed comfortably. I knew the feeling. It felt much better, just being in here. I put the skein of yarn I'd used to fix my sock on one of my shelves and spotted some white, puffy fabric that reminded me of marshmallow goo, which then reminded me of the goo I got on Grace's flute case. I felt bad about that.

But it gave me an idea. I'd make Grace a flute cover to protect her flute. I went to the shelf I'd labeled FABRICS. I found this silver material that reminded me so much of a flute I couldn't resist. I measured it and cut it to be about flute-sized.

I went over to my sewing machine, which was tucked into the back of my closet.

It was white, but I'd decorated it with some shiny turquoise, silver, and red bling, so it was really cute now.

I sewed the white fabric into the silver material to make a lining that gave a nod to the marshmallow-goo fiasco and was thick and puffy enough to protect the flute. Then, for personalization, I found a little rose-colored *G* patch from my alphabet collection, and I ironed it on.

I turned it over in my hands. I liked how it turned out. I hoped Grace would like it, too. I heard a knock at my bedroom door. Then footsteps.

"Hi, honey." Mom stuck her head in. "It's getting late. I made some popcorn for you."

"Thanks. Want to see what I made?" I said, holding up the flute cover.

"That's very pretty," my mom said. "What's the G stand for?"

"Kind of a friend I made today," I said. "She's really into her flute, so I made her this case."

"I'm glad you're making new friends," Mom said.

"Taylor met her first," I said. "She looks more like Taylor than me, if you were wondering. Normal."

"Honey, that's not what I was thinking." Mom sighed. "I'd be happy if you made some friends who dressed creatively like you. I admire your artistic streak and hope you find others who have that, too. As long as they respect their mothers and aren't regulars in detention."

"Well, don't even worry about it. I didn't even see anyone who remotely dressed like me. You'd think from six middle schools, I wouldn't be the only one."

"Well, hon"—Mom sighed—"we aren't exactly living in the hub of fashion-forwardness here. I do really like your flute cover. I'm guessing your new friend will, too."

"Thanks," I said. "And thanks for the popcorn."

I wheeled my chair over to my desk and turned on my computer. It was slow but did the job. I clicked in my private password and watched as my background on my Facebook page popped up. It was currently pink and red. I'd collaged pictures of different kinds of shoes all over it.

My iChat popped up.

TayterTot: r u busy?
I replied:
LyVin: no wuts up?
TayterTot: trying to pick an outfit for 2morro.
HELP!! ???

I smiled. I had some ideas.

N ice skirt," someone next to me snickered as I headed to my locker after last period.

I caught a glimpse of her. I could have told her that that shade of green made her skin look yellowish. She really should go with a deeper shade of green. Or ooh! Aquamarine would really bring out the shine in her hair. If she was a nice person, we might have become friends and I could have helped her with that. Her loss!

I'd survived another day of school and was actually looking forward to opening up my locker. And when I did, I smiled.

Last night after I'd given Taylor some clothes ideas, my mind had been racing with inspiration. I'd hit my closet and come up with some things to decorate my locker. I found grass green shag fabric to line the inside shelves. Then I'd found a box of fake deep pink carnations I'd randomly bought at a craft store. I'd cut a Styrofoam board to the size of my locker door and glued on a round mirror and a sparkly frame with a picture of Bella wearing a pink tutu. I stuck in the carnations, surrounding it like a wall of flowers. I'd sticky-tacked all of them in my locker this morning, hung a little floral air freshener, and ta-da! A garden, a little bit of outside brought in. A space of my own in this impersonal and unoriginal school. Okay, that sounded dorky. But seriously, it looked cool.

"Whoa," a voice next to me said. "That's some locker."

Locker guy. His hotness had not subsided. He was wearing an olive green T-shirt, a white button-down over it, and yes—the green sneakers.

"Yes," I blurted. "I mean, thanks!"

Yeeps.

"How's your sock thing?" he asked.

"You saved its life," I told him. "I was able to knit it back together."

"You made them yourself?" he asked me.

"Yeah," I said. "But I guess not so well, since they fell apart but . . ."

"Still, that's impressive," he said.

I blanked on what to say, so I stuck my head in my locker and pretended to get my books. The guy turned back to his locker, got his stuff, and then shut the door.

"Um!" I blurted out, before he could leave. "I really like your sneakers."

"Yeah?" he said, looking down. "I wasn't sure if they

were too crazy, but there's something about them. I saw them on the shelf and they just, I don't know."

"Called out to you?" I suggested.

"Yeah." He smiled. "That's it. The sneakers just called my name. Which is Jacob, by the way."

"I'm Lynn," I said.

"I have to go. So, I'll see you at the locker, Lynn," he said.

I angled my locker door so I could catch a glimpse of him in my mirror, walking down the hallway.

"Ahem!" A voice from behind startled me. Taylor was standing there with her hands on her hips and not looking too happy. "Aren't you supposed to be meeting me at *my* locker? You're late."

"I'm sorry—" I said.

"I'm kidding," Taylor said. "You're only like two minutes late. And obviously you have a good excuse."

"Um, what?" I said.

"Hello, flirting with Cute Locker Boy?" Taylor leaned next to my locker and grinned.

"I wasn't flirting," I said, reddening. "I was just thanking him."

"For hotness? For giving you eye candy at your locker?" Taylor asked.

"No, he's the one who helped me when my sock snagged at FonDo yesterday." I shut my locker.

"Oooh," Taylor said. "So, do you think there's any potential?"

"What? Me and him?" I said. "Hello? Did you see him? Cute? Normal? The anti-me?"

"Oh come on, you're cute," Taylor said. "Obviously not normal but . . ."

"Quit while you're ahead," I suggested as the final bell rang.

"Wait, that was the bell for the buses," Taylor said. "Did you just miss yours? Does that mean what I think it means?"

"No, it doesn't mean I changed my mind and I'm going to FonDo with you," I said. "Dex has the car and he's giving me a ride home. But thanks for reminding me that I have something for you to give Grace for me."

I'd decided it wasn't a good idea to go to FonDo again, even if I'd liked it up until the whole unraveling sock fiasco.

"You have fun," I said.

"Hmm." Taylor smirked, looking pointedly at my outfit. "What's your outfit about today?"

"Just stuff," I said, but half-smiled when Taylor raised an eyebrow.

Oh, okay. I had cut off the sleeves of the pale green sweater and added cream fishnet stockings on my arms to replace them, giving the effect, I thought, of lacy Swiss cheese, my favorite fondue. But hopefully not too cheesy. I had on a cocoa-colored skirt as an ode to the chocolate fondue, and had sewed lace doilies onto it to complement the lacy Swiss cheese look. And my tall chocolate brown boots.

"Maybe FonDo did inspire me a little bit," I admitted. "I didn't think it was obvious."

"The bracelets you made from the chocolate wrappers tipped me off," Taylor said. "You're sure you don't want to go to FonDo?"

I was relieved to see Dex walking toward me to officially mark the end of my day.

"Change of plans, Lynn," Dex said. "I just got called in to cover someone's shift at FonDo. So, go with Taylor."

"Yeees!" Taylor pumped her fist in the air. "Fate has intervened! We'll see you there, Dex!"

I followed after her, defeated.

"Okay, so according to my sources, it's cool to order a skinny mochaccino, a skim vanilla latte, or a bubble tea," Taylor said. "But not the FonDo Fiesta. I wondered how Arin Morgan went there after school every day and still stayed so thin. No wonder I'm such a fat cow."

"Stop it," I said.

"I am going to stop eating. I'm getting bubble tea," Taylor said. "Or do the bubbles have calories?"

"No, not stop eating, I meant, stop saying you're fat," I told her.

"Hello, Miss Fashion, you know which pants are coming back in style? It's like the fashion people asked themselves: Which style will make round girls look the most bulgy? Ha-ha, we'll torture them with that."

"Well, if you don't like them, don't wear them," I said.

"Oh, but I have to," Taylor said. "Hang on, I'll show you."

Taylor took out her cell and looked something up.

"See?" she said. "Here are the must-have pants of the

coming season. I found them on three trend sites, so it's a given."

I looked over her shoulder. They *were* cute, if you were six feet tall and a supermodel.

"I know I can't bug you every night about what to wear," Taylor said. "So I'm going to figure it all out myself. I'm going to be a fashionista if it kills me. I'm devoting three hours a night to fashion blogs and *Teen Vogue*-ing."

"I really don't mind if you call me for advice," I told her.

"Thanks," Taylor said. "I just figure it's about time I learn to dress myself."

"Three hours a night?" I said.

"Not enough, is it?" Taylor sighed. "I probably need four."

"No, I meant three hours is too much," I said. "Hello? Homework? If you flunk out of school, your style's not going to matter much."

"I took this 'What's your personal style?' quiz online. I came out Completely Confused Couture. And it's true. By the time I figure out a trend, it's over," Taylor said, her voice rising higher.

"Taylor, chill," I said.

"You wouldn't understand," Taylor said. "You breathe fashion. Even though you wear that, you put together normal outfits for me in a second. It comes easy to you. You love it."

Well, I wouldn't say it came easy for me. But I did love it. I loved *Project Runway* reruns and the Style Network. I read teen fashionista blogs and style blogs and was obsessed with making virtual collections on Polyvore. I also flipped through European *Vogue*s at the bookstore to see what would come to America next. I watched YouTube videos of Fashion Weeks all over the world.

I'd always been like that. When I had to do a biography report in third grade, I'd done it on Coco Chanel. I did a history paper on fashion trends through the decades.

Fashion was my thing. But I did it all for fun. It relaxed me, inspired me, excited me. Taylor didn't look relaxed, inspired, or excited. She just looked overwhelmed.

"This time I'm going to be on trend," Taylor was saying. "Maybe not ahead of them like you, but in the know, at least.

"I had hoped high school would be different," Taylor continued miserably. "But I'm still totally a nobody. I'm not a swimmer, cheerleader, or lacrosse star. I don't star in plays. I'm in band but practically in last chair. I'm like a nobody who is good at nothing."

Taylor walked faster and held the door open for me.

"That's so not true," I said. "You're the nicest person I know."

"Whoopee," Taylor said.

I was quiet. I mean, in a way she was right. Being nice seems like it should be the most important thing. Then I thought about the Chaseys of the world. Being nice doesn't get you much of anywhere in ninth grade.

"You wouldn't understand." Taylor was still talking.

"You can sew, make cool things, you have your own thing going. I have nothing going for me. Except this."

Taylor reached into her bag and flashed some platinum at me.

"My mom gave me the credit card," Taylor said. "Part of her master plan for me to be a Chasey chaser. With this and my new fashion genius, I'll at least look good doing nothing."

"Just come on, maybe a snack will cheer you up," I sighed.

"No snack," Taylor said. "Don't forget those pants I have to wear this winter."

We walked along in silence until we were at the front door of FonDo.

Taylor pushed open the front door. The place was packed. I saw my brother in his server uniform running around like a crazy guy. I noticed that Chasey was at our old booth. Taylor noticed the same thing and we both headed toward the back. Grace was at almost the same table next to the girls' room.

"I tried to get a better table," Grace apologized.

"Oh, don't worry, this seems like *our* area now," I told her. We slid into our seats. Being in the back meant that I was less likely to unravel in front of a crowd again anyway. Which reminded me . . .

"I'm sorry about the marshmallow I spilled on your case," I told Grace. "So, I have this for you."

I took a deep breath and pulled out a paper bag I'd put the flute case in. I slid it across the table to her.

"What's this?" Grace looked at us.

Taylor shrugged. "Don't look at me."

"It's no biggie, just something I made," I said. Grace opened the bag. She pulled out the flute case and looked at it.

"It's a flute case," I explained. I felt a little embarrassed. I mean, I hardly knew her. Maybe she'd hate it. Maybe flutes didn't even go in cases.

"Ooh," Grace said. "That's beautiful."

"I love that!" Taylor said.

"You really like it? I'll make you one, too," I said to her. I smiled at their reactions.

"Oh, you don't have to," Taylor said. "But if you did, make it pink."

"I can't believe you made this," Grace said, turning it over in her hands. "This is amazing."

"It's so not a big deal," I said, feeling slightly embarrassed about the fuss. I leaned back in my chair and knocked into the person sitting behind me.

I turned around to see an emo girl wearing a hoodie that was a knockoff from a retro eighties line of clothes.

"Sorry," I said to her. The girl nodded and started to turn back, but I kept talking.

"Um, about your shirt? I know a vintage site online that sells the original stuff really cheap."

The girl raised her pierced eyebrow. Then she turned back around.

Alrighty then. Just trying to be helpful.

"I wish we could do this every day after school," Grace

sighed. "But my parents are on me about my homework, chamber music practice, and practicing my piano."

"And my mom's making me do these heinous tumbling and hip-hop classes," Taylor said. "She's convinced I have a shot at making cheerleading. She hasn't figured out you need coordination to do these things."

I patted her on the shoulder. I'd watched her try out last year and yeah, it was painful.

"What do you take after school?" Grace asked me.

"I'm pretty open. I have to concentrate on school stuff," I said. I hadn't really seen anything at school I wanted to do. I wasn't brave enough to try art club, plus there weren't any late buses near my house. And my mom didn't have a lot of time for the driving-me-around-to-classes thing.

"Well, I have Mondays free," Grace said.

"Let's make that our thing!" Taylor said. "Mondays at FonDo."

All of a sudden a pen and napkin appeared on the table in front of me. I looked up. The emo girl from the table behind me was standing there.

"Hi!" Taylor said brightly. "I'm Taylor."

The emo girl glanced at her and then at me.

"It's called VintageBette," I said to the girl as I wrote the website name on the napkin. She took it and walked away.

"What was that about?" Taylor asked.

"This website I think she'll like," I said. I watched the emo girl go back to her table.

I looked around at the scene. People were hanging out laughing, talking, chilling.

Yeah, we were at possibly the worst table in the place. But so what. I looked at Taylor and Grace and smiled as I sipped my hot chocolate. I looked down at my FonDo-inspired outfit and felt totally right.

All of a sudden, the buzz from the front got louder and louder. I leaned forward and saw a group of girls walking around in the front, handing out flyers. They were wearing matching black T-shirts with lettering on them. I could tell it was a website, but www . . . ?

"I wonder what the flyers say," Taylor said. "We'll see when they get back here."

But when the girls got about halfway to the back, they stopped passing out the flyers. We watched them leave the café.

"They must have run out," Grace said.

"I'm kind of curious," Taylor admitted. "Lynn, do you think your brother knows?"

I got up and walked to the front where my brother was cleaning off some tables. Girls were squealing and reading the flyers.

"Hey, Dex," I said. "What were those flyers? We didn't get any in the back."

"You mean those flyers the hot chicks were passing out?" Dex said. He pulled a crumpled paper out of his back pocket and handed it to me. "I took one in case it was for a party with them."

"Can I borrow this?" I asked Dex. I didn't wait for his answer. I walked quickly back to our table and placed the flyer down on it.

"Check this out," I said.

"Ooh, I love *GlITter Girl* magazine!" Taylor said, reading. "Did you see the latest cover with the new American Idols on it?"

"It could be a scam," Grace warned. "Like, be a model or just look like one, but we'll take your money no matter what. Let me check their site." Grace pulled out a phone and started clicking.

I watched the girls up front talking and waving the flyers around.

"Yup, it's for real," Grace said. "I went to the *GlITter Girl* site, and it says they're launching a new online magazine because trends are happening so fast! Up-to-the-minute fashion, it says."

"Trends are happening too fast for me, that's for sure," sighed Taylor. "I mean, like these pants? Weren't they just in? Are they out already and nobody told me?"

Um. Well, yes.

"So the magazine is traveling the country going to different cities looking for teens to help them spot trends," Grace continued, reading from the site. "And the audition is Saturday morning at nine, at the mall."

"I wonder why they're coming here," I mused. "It's not like we're a fashion capital of the world. Or the state. Or anywhere."

It was true. We lived in a small town in Pennsylvania. It seemed like everyone pretty much wore the same thing, except me, of course. We definitely weren't known for our cutting-edge trendiness.

"Maybe they want a taste of regular people," Taylor said. "We're about as regular as we can get. Except you, of course, Lynn."

"It says there will be people from *GlITter Girl* and special guest Valentyna," Grace read off the screen.

"Valentyna will be there?" I asked. "Valentyna with a *y*?"

"Yes," Grace said. "You know who she is?"

"Totally," I told them. "She's a fashion designer. An icon."

"Like Marc Jacobs, Ralph Lauren, and Juicy Couture," Taylor added

"Uh, Taylor? Juicy Couture isn't someone's name," I informed her.

"Ohhh, that's good," she said. "It would stink to be named Juicy."

Taylor, Grace, Chasey, and I all laughed. Wait a minute. Chasey? Chasey apparently had been walking by our table and stopped.

"I'm laughing not only because that girl thinks Juicy is a person, but because Liz is holding one of the flyers," Chasey said loudly.

I tried not to flinch.

"Who's Liz?" Grace whispered.

"Didn't Liz notice they didn't even pass out those flyers back here?" Chasey continued. "They knew the kind of people they're looking for are the kind of people that get front row seats at FonDo. Not in the back. By the bathroom."

"She probably scared them away with that outfit," Kyla giggled.

They cracked up as they went inside the girls' room. We all looked down at our plates for a moment, until I cleared my throat.

"Um, well," I said. "That was embarrassing. I'm sorry you guys got dissed by association because of me. I should just go."

"Yes, you should. And we'll go with you to support you," Taylor said.

I stood up, but Taylor and Grace remained seated.

"Uh, guys?" I said. "Aren't we going?"

"I didn't mean go *now*," Taylor said. "I meant go to the *GlITter Girl* auditions so you can try out. Sit down."

"Wait, what?" I asked, sitting back down. "No way. I have enough humiliation in my life. Hello, you guys just witnessed it?"

"Oh, come on, it would be great," Taylor said. "If you get on the trend-spotting panel, you'll get all the inside scoops first! You'll know what's going to be in before everyone else."

"Look at me," I said. "If I really just cared about what was 'in,' would I wear this? This shirt style won't be in for another, oh, eight months or so. My earrings may never be in—but I love them. I'm not about what's in, and that's what they want. So, discussion over."

"Discussion so not over," Taylor said. "Remember how you were saying you wanted to find your people? People who would appreciate your creativity and uniqueness because nobody here was getting you? Maybe this is your chance, Lynn."

Hmm—I mean I'd had my moments of thinking I might have people out there, like while watching *Project Runway* or getting the random supportive comment on my Polyvore collections online. But could it happen here, in my town?

Taylor and Grace looked at me hopefully.

"Your people, Lynn," Taylor said. "Just imagine if you were on the IT panel. Do it for all of us, Lynn. For the little people who get trompled on."

They both looked at me. And I slowly nodded.

After that, I couldn't back out. I mean, I seriously *couldn't*, but I tried. But Taylor was not taking no for an answer. I told her I was sneezing, probably getting a cold. Taylor told me to decorate a tissue box just in case. Next day, I told her I was starting to feel like I was going to puke. Which was actually true.

"You can puke in my tote bag if you have to," Taylor said.

So Friday night, I was a mixture of nerves and excitement. Maybe, just maybe, Taylor was right. I'd meet people who were at least a little more like me at the auditions. Like the people who put together the styles on the runway that nobody would really wear in public but were the talk of the fashion industry. Like the people who were on the cutting edge, not just on the edge like me. I pictured a line of girls who were all dressed in their own unique styles, admiring each other instead of mocking each other.

And suddenly, I felt inspired. I would make something new. Something that called out to me.

I grinned as I thought of Jacob at his locker talking about his shoes. Okay, I would make some shoes that, too, called my name. I clicked onto iTunes and brought up my Fashion Inspiration Playlist. I went to my closet and pulled out a pair of white pumps and a pair of tan wedge shoes. Boring—but not for long. I took the heel off the white pumps and detached the wedge from the other shoes. I glued the wedge to the bottom of the white shoe. I liked the look so far—a chunky wedge base yet a delicate top. A high heel, but not so high I couldn't walk.

Very cool. But they needed more. I went into my closet and looked around. I looked at the collage of pictures on my inspiration board. Pictures of fashions, pictures of creations I'd made. Pictures of styles I'd put together. Pictures of me and Taylor, my mom, Bella. Ticket stubs from concerts I'd been to. Random pictures of beaches and flowers and designs that had caught my eye.

Hmm.

I took off some of the things on my bulletin board. I scanned them in, shrunk them until they were tiny, and printed them out. I got some of my fashion magazines and cut out some words. TRUTH. REAL. ORIGINAL. Then I dug around in the box and found some sequins and attached those, too. Then I went to my closet and pulled out my box of craft supplies. I grabbed some glue and carefully decorated the shoes with the tiny pictures.

I held up the shoes. They needed just a little more. I painted the soles of my shoes a bright yellow.

Oh yes, those shoes were . . . it. So totally and completely me. I loved loved loved my shoes. They were seriously awesome. I'd never made anything so . . . so . . . perfect.

Bella came over and snuggled up next to me.

"You like my shoes?" I asked her as I scratched her under the lavender sweater threaded with gold that I'd made for her. "When there's a Doggy IT panel, you're definitely in."

Bella barked in agreement. And then a minute later my door opened and my mom stuck her head in, looking half asleep.

"Did I just hear Bella bark?" she asked, yawning. Then her eyes widened. "Lynn Ivy Vincent! Are you still up making things? It's almost one thirty in the morning!"

Whoops.

"Oops," I said, trying to sound apologetic. "Sorry, Mom. I lost track of time."

"Go to bed," Mom grumbled. But she blew me a kiss as she left.

I put Bella on my bed and turned off my music. I took out a thin purple permanent marker and wrote in small letters on the yellow soles: LyVin. Then I put the shoes on my desk where they wouldn't smudge. They looked very cool. If they were dry in the morning, I might even wear them to the audition. Which was in eight hours. Yeeps. I went to bed and tried to calm my racing mind.

Y ou're number two thirteen." A woman dressed in a
blue suit handed me a sticker that said HELLO MY
NAME IS #213.

"I'm just here for moral support," Taylor said when the
woman tried to give her a sticker, too.

I looked around at the line of girls snaking through the
mall. Some girls at the front of the line had sleeping bags.

"I guess we weren't first," I said. "I think those girls
slept here overnight."

"Oh, well," Taylor said. "I'm sure it doesn't matter if
you're first or two thirteen. I'm sure everyone has an
equal chance."

"I'm sure it'll all be one big blur by the time they meet
me," I said.

"Nah, you stand out," Taylor said.

I looked around and sighed. My vision of girls in their most creative outfits was way off base. Instead, I was surrounded by adorable girls in adorable outfits, but more along the lines of AE/Hollister/Abercrombie. Some Juicy, Ed Hardy and a lot of designer bags. I looked at them and thought, *Totally on trend and very cute.*

I was wearing a white T-shirt. I'd fastened on skinny black suspenders. I'd flung on a superlong yellow-and-black scarf I'd knitted. A very full black layered skirt I'd made that poufed out. Thick yellow tights. Thrifted violet opera gloves that went up past my elbows. I'd put on a silvery crocheted sequin beret. I'd wanted to shine a little bit like a Glitter Girl, and the sequins were like little mirrors, reflecting the fashions of the girls around me. Underneath the skirt, I'd put some denim shorts, on which I'd glued a patch shaped like a heart in a secret nod to Valentyna. I saw in an interview once that, like a valentine, Valentyna put a heart after her name on all of her labels as a play on her name.

But the best part, of course, was going to be the shoes. My new creation made me happy. My shoes had dried pretty well overnight, but they were still a little wet. So I was keeping them in a shoebox till the last minute and had a pair of regular green Chucks on for now.

"Come on, show me the shoes," Taylor said.

"Okay, but promise if you hate them you won't say anything," I said. I'd gotten kind of attached to the shoes.

I took a deep breath and opened the shoebox.

Silence. Taylor was just standing there looking into the box without reacting.

Doo doo doo.

"Okay, you hate them." I shut the box lid.

"What? No! I'm still looking. There's so much to look at," Taylor said. She grabbed the box from me and opened the lid. She held the box far away from her face. Then she held it up close.

"Whoa," she said.

"Whoa good or whoa bad?" I ventured.

"Good whoa," Taylor said emphatically. "Lynn, omigosh, this shoe is just so . . . Like, whoa. Beautiful. Amazing. It's so cool how from far away they just look like colors and designs," Taylor went on. "Then you look up close and it's like, whoa! All these little pictures. Hey! It's a little me! You put *me* on your shoe!"

Yay.

"You *have* to wear these now," Taylor said. "And then you have to go home and make me a pair."

I smiled and pulled one of the shoes out of the box. And I got a lump in my throat. I'd been working so hard in my closet for so long, and I'd never worked on anything like these shoes. I'd made them so *me*. I felt like I'd captured myself in them.

"Photo op," Taylor said, holding up her cell. "Let me capture the debut of the shoes."

She stood by me and recorded a video.

"We're here at the *GlITter Girl* IT panel audition,"

Taylor reported. "Check out Lynn's shoe. It rocks!"

"I do love my shoe!" I said, smiling. Taylor asked the girl behind us to take a picture. We put our arms around each other, and I held up the shoe as we posed.

"Thanks," Taylor said, and put her cell back in her bag. "Look, some girls are coming out. Do they look happy or freaked out?"

I watched as some of the first girls came out after their audition. I watched them pose, as if they were celebrities walking the red carpet instead of past a line of other girls.

"They look happy," I sighed. "And also familiar. It's Chasey and crew."

They were coming closer, so I shoved the shoe in the box and replaced the lid.

"I rocked it," I heard Chasey say as she got closer. "I am so in."

Don't see me or Taylor. Don't see me or Taylor.

"Oh, *ew*," Chasey said under her breath, obviously seeing Taylor and me.

For a brief and glorious moment, I thought she was just going to walk by and ignore us.

"Hi, Chasey!" Taylor blurted out. She paused and then held up her hand lamely for a high five. "Fellow Independence High Schoolers!"

Chasey looked at Taylor's hand, left hanging in the air.

"I'm surprised to see you two here. I didn't know you two even knew where the mall was," Chasey said. "I thought you bought your clothes at the Salvation Army,

Taylor. And Lynn, well. Does what you're wearing even count as clothes? People are, like, staring at you."

I glanced at Taylor, who was biting her lip.

"You're right, Chasey," I said, stepping closer to her. "People *are* staring at me. And they probably think you're friends with me. Look, the woman from the IT panel is looking at us. She probably thinks we're one happy clique."

"What?" Chasey said, backing away from me. She raised her voice a little bit. "We're so not friends with them, if anybody's wondering."

And a split second later Chasey, Kayden, and Kyla were gone.

"Nice job stopping them from insulting us," Taylor said admiringly.

"I'd feel more victorious if I didn't have to insult myself to do it," I said. "Telling her she'd be associated with me sent her running."

"Erg," Taylor said. "I *just* thought of a comeback. I hate that. I never think of anything to say until after she's gone."

"It wouldn't make any difference if you did," I told Taylor, watching them walk away. "She doesn't care what we say to her, just what she says to us. We're just pawns in her quest for world domination. Anyway, she's gone. I'm going to put on my new shoes and let them protect me from the Chaseys of the world."

I didn't want anything to shake my confidence today.

I took my shoes out of the box. I pulled off my Chucks

and put on the new shoes. I stuck out my foot to check the shoe out.

"Cool shoes," a girl walking by said.

"Oh! Thanks!" I said. I looked up to see if she was being sarcastic, but she looked sincere.

Well, that was nice. I smiled as I looked down at my shoes. Then I noticed something. Uh-oh, the glue wasn't totally dry on one of the shoes. The little picture of me and Taylor was peeling off. I stuck it back on and patted it down. It fell off. Shoot.

"What's wrong?" Taylor asked me.

"Now my shoe is coming unglued," I said. I patted the picture again until it stuck down. As I stood up, I tucked my hair behind my ear and . . .

Argh.

"Oh great, I have glue stuck to my fingers," I told Taylor, as I attempted to detach my fingers from each other. "And I just wiped it in my hair. Can you tell?"

"Erm, no! No," Taylor said. "Well, yeah. Part of your bangs are kind of glued to your forehead, and then the piece over your ear is sticking out. Then there's your eyebrow—"

"I'm going to run to the bathroom and wash it off," I said. "Can you please stay here and hold my place?"

"The line is barely moving, but hurry up," Taylor said. "It makes me nervous."

I grabbed my bag and walked through the mall to the bathrooms. Oh great. There was a line going out the girls' room door. I got in line and waited, wondering if I could skip the line, since I didn't really have to go. I just wanted to wash my hair and hands off.

"Um, excuse me, I just need to wash my—" I started to say, trying to inch forward.

"No ditching," the girl in front of me said.

When I finally got into the bathroom, I washed the glue off as best as I could. I tried to put my hair and right eyebrow back into a seminormal position and hoped they weren't looking for perfect supermodels. I came out and headed back toward the line, looking for Taylor. I looked and looked until I saw Taylor waving like a crazy person. Omigosh, she was at the front of the line! I rushed over to her.

"She's here! That's her! Number two thirteen!" Taylor was saying to a girl holding a clipboard.

"I'm sorry, but we called that group," the girl said. "Step aside."

"But I just had to go to the bathroom," I protested.

"No exceptions," the girl said.

"Pretty please?" Taylor pleaded. "She had a fashion emergency."

"Step aside," she said. She raised her voice and called out. "Next group, please, numbers two twenty to two thirty!"

And that was that.

I stood there for a second. And then stepped aside.

My shoes had betrayed me. Okay, no, I had betrayed myself. I had deluded myself into thinking I could get to go into the audition. And even if I hadn't been picked, maybe even for a brief minute or two, I could have talked fashion for a little while with real fashion people. I could have breathed the same air as Valentyna. That would have been enough. Honestly.

But now, nothing.

Taylor and I walked in silence away from the crowd of girls and toward the escalators.

"We could try again," Taylor said. "Come on, just go back in line."

We both looked at the long line of confident, well-dressed girls.

"No," I said. "It was a sign. I'm done. Let's just go home."

Actually, my shoes had probably saved me from the pain of rejection. Because what if I went in there and they all laughed at me? *What if the editors, what if Valentyna, who knows fashion, gave me the look?* The look that said, What is that girl wearing and why does she have to be such a freak? It probably was fate stepping in, after all.

"Sorry, we're stuck here," Taylor said. "My mom's still getting her nails done upstairs. So while I feel your pain, we have to wait till she calls us. Maybe we can get something to eat in the deli?"

I sighed. I followed Taylor into the deli. It was pretty much empty, and we sat down in one of the booths.

"I really need to go to the bathroom," Taylor said. "Want to come?"

"I've had enough of bathrooms right now," I said. I slumped on the seat as she walked toward the girls' room. I felt really, really tired, and not just because I'd been up so late last night. I peeled off my opera gloves. Ripped off the beret. Tore off my suspenders, skirt, and scarf. I tossed them all in my bag. Now I just had the white tee and denim shorts on. I tried to peel off the little heart patch from the shorts that I'd glued on as a secret nod to Valentyna, but for once something I'd glued *did* stick. Figures. I gave up on it and looked in the mirror.

Now in the T-shirt and shorts I looked as blah, unoriginal, and boring as I felt. I reached down to pull off my shoes. I didn't even want to look at those right now; I just wanted all memory of this day erased. I pulled off one of them and then started to pull off the other. But it was stuck. Oh great, it was stuck to my tights. The glue had struck again.

Ugh. I totally and completely gave up. I lay my head down on my arms on the table.

"Excuse me, miss?" I heard a server say above me. "Can I get you something while you're waiting?"

Yes, you can get me a new life. I'd like to order a plain, boring, everyday life. I raised my head.

"A glass of ice water, please," I said. I leaned over to see if Taylor was coming back, and that's when I saw her. And by her, I didn't mean Taylor, I meant *her.*

Valentyna!

Valentyna! The real Valentyna was sitting in the booth a little ways down from me. I almost fell out of my own booth. I looked closer to make sure I wasn't imagining things, but it was definitely her. She was wearing all black, with a signature yellow-and-silver scarf wrapped around her head. And oh! I could see her shoes under the table. They were encrusted with jewels and they were so . . . so . . . incredible. . . . And she had a little black Malti-poo seated next to her! I knew that dog! It was Pasha, her constant companion at fashion shows and in life. I couldn't believe it. *The* Valentyna was here in this very same room as me.

As I was gaping at Valentyna, Taylor came out and walked right by her, oblivious. She slid into our booth.

"Taylor! Do you know who you just passed?" I hissed.

Taylor turned around to look. "Oooh, cute puppy. That's weird they'd let a dog in the deli."

"Not the cute dog," I whispered. "That's Valentyna! *The* Valentyna!

"No way!" Taylor said. "She does look very stylish. Hey, did you change your clothes? What are you wearing?"

"That's so not important right now." I waved her off. "I can't believe I can see the real Valentyna," I said. "I thought I'd missed my chance when I couldn't audition."

"Get closer," Taylor urged. "Go to the bathroom and walk by her so you can see her close up."

"No," I said. "I can't. I can't. Can I? No, I can't."

"Lynn," Taylor said. She looked me in the eye. "Go to the bathroom. Now!"

I would. I had nothing to lose, just walking by her casually to the girls' room. It wasn't like she was going to look up and notice me. She would have no clue that once upon a time I thought I had a chance to audition. Now I was just a normal girl in the deli.

I stood up.

"Lynn, you're only wearing one shoe," Taylor pointed out. "The floor's a little gross in the bathroom."

Oh yeah. I reached under the table and slid my other shoe back on.

"You're ready," Taylor said. "Go for it, Lynn."

I casually walked toward the bathroom. Just walking, walking like a regular girl would. As I walked past her booth, I heard Valentyna order some corned beef for her dog. I got a quick sneak peek at her outfit as I breezed by.

I pushed the girls' room door open and grinned as I went inside. The rest of the disastrous day melted away as it sunk in that I'd just seen Valentyna in real life. I caught a glimpse of myself smiling in the mirror. Oh, my glue head was back. Random pieces of my hair were sticking up, and I pretty much looked ridiculous. I went back out into the deli and walked quickly, keeping my head down, staying as invisible as possible. Walking, walking, walking near Valentyna, walking past her, walking, walking past the server holding Pasha's corned beef and—

Ack! Tripping! And losing my balance! I completely tripped and then, okay, I'm not sure exactly what happened. Taylor said she saw me going facedown and kicking my leg up. And then she saw my shoe flying across the deli.

And landing on Valentyna's table.

I turned around and gasped. My shoe had landed on Valentyna's salad plate. Lettuce and tomatoes and salad pieces were flying in the air. I heard Valentyna let out a little shriek, and I heard Pasha bark.

After that, I didn't hear or see a thing. I just ran out of the deli in horror.

ynn, you look . . . different," Grace said to me as I sat down in the seat next to her at our table at FonDo.

I was wearing what was possibly the most shocking outfit I'd ever worn: a plain navy shirt. Jeans. Regular white sneakers. And my hair in a ponytail tied with a rubber band.

Yes, I was dressed like everyone else. Actually, I was dressed more boring than everyone. As I'd walked through FonDo after school, nobody looked at me, nobody noticed me. And that was going to be my new look.

Invisible. I was planning to stay anonymous for the rest of my life.

"I'm wearing the regular clothing of a regular person," I said, shrugging. "No big deal."

"Sorry we're late," Taylor said to Grace, sliding into the booth. "I had to convince Lynn to come here."

Convince? Taylor had practically held on to my jacket until I'd missed the bus. I hadn't been in the mood to come to FonDo today. I can't say that I was feeling very sociable.

"I tried IMing you this weekend a couple times to see how the audition went," Grace said to me. "But you were never online."

Yeah, that. That was because I'd spent the rest of the weekend in bed with the covers pulled over my head, trying to erase the image of my flying shoe meeting Valentyna's salad.

But okay, around midnight last night I'd finally cracked just a little. I'd gone on the audition website to skim the IT panel list. Obviously I wasn't going to be on it. But there were two names I recognized. Arin Morgan and Chasey Welch. Both of whom were also sitting here at FonDo, sitting in the front where the IT people sat; particularly the IT people for the *GlITter Girls* panel.

"Well, the audition didn't go as we hoped," Taylor said, with forced cheeriness. "But Lynn gave it a good try and I'm proud of her."

"Oh be quiet," I grumbled. "Just tell her. I got rejected before I even auditioned; I covered myself in glue and then I threw my shoe at Valentyna."

Grace's mouth fell wide open.

"She didn't throw her shoe," Taylor reassured her. "She tripped and it flew off. Unfortunately it landed on Valentyna's lunch."

"So let's move forward, shall we?" I said, ignoring

Grace's confusion. "No need to focus on me. Grace, how was *your* weekend?"

Before she had a chance to answer, Grace's cell phone beeped. She read her text message.

"Oh no, I have to leave already," Grace said. "My mother apparently scheduled an extra piano lesson to prepare for my recital. That about sums up my weekend—studying, practice, studying. But really, Lynn, I'm sorry about your audition."

"Thanks," I said. "Really, it's no big deal."

We said bye to Grace as a waiter-not-Dex came over. Taylor ordered bubble tea. I ordered a diet soda.

"So, what's new in Taylorland?" I asked.

"Well," Taylor said. "Not much. Except I have a best friend whose personality has dramatically changed in the last forty-eight hours. And she's wearing clothes more out of style than mine. I mean, weren't those the gym shoes your mother bought you in, like, seventh grade?"

I looked down. Yes. Yes, they were.

"Speaking of shoes, what did you do with the shoe?" Taylor said.

"You mean the other shoe that I *didn't* fling at Valentyna?" I asked her. Taylor nodded.

"I threw it in the trash," I told her.

"Lynn!" Taylor protested. "You threw that shoe in the trash? I loved that shoe! You should've kept it! You should've at least given it to me."

"Taylor, can we please talk about something else?" I asked. "I'm trying to block that disaster out of my memory.

I never want to hear about that shoe. In fact, please delete that video you took with me and the shoe."

"Lynn," Taylor protested. Then she saw the look on my face and pulled out her phone. "Okay, if you're sure."

"I'm sure. I want all traces of the shoe gone. And I will be happy never to speak of Valentyna, or the IT panel, or anything related to fashion ever again."

"Don't you think you're overreacting just a little?" Taylor said. "Should I start worrying about you?"

"Nope." I shrugged. "I'm fine."

"She's not fine," my brother said. Dex was standing over our table with our drinks. He put them on the table and continued. "Lynn stayed in her room all weekend. Not only that, she was listening to the pop music station. I could hear it through the walls."

"What's wrong with that?" I protested. "Everyone listens to pop stations."

"Everyone except you," Dex said. "You discover new bands on iTunes and on obscure indie websites."

"I used to," I said. "Past tense."

"I can't believe it," Dex said. "My sister has turned normal."

Dex shook his head and walked off.

Taylor and I sat and drank our drinks. I looked up front and watched all the action.

"I hate to wuss out on you," I said. "But I think I just want to go home."

"Okay." Taylor sighed. "I can see you're hopeless today. I'll call my mother to come get us."

We packed up our stuff as Taylor called her mom.

"She said to wait outside," Taylor said, getting up.

I followed her, and kept my eyes to the ground as I passed the booth where Chasey and her people were sitting.

"Is that Liz?" a voice called out loudly. Chasey slid her feet out of her booth so they were in the aisle. "Whoa, it *is* Liz. I so didn't recognize you. You almost look normal. Well, your clothes anyway."

"Yes, hello," I said, stepping over her feet. "You can go back to ignoring me now."

"You look so different from when I saw you going into the IT panel. Oh, that reminds me, I'm *so* sorry neither of you made it." Chasey did a fairly good impression of someone being sad.

"Sure, whatever," I said. I tried to keep moving, but she stood up and blocked me.

"I've already got my first IT panel assignment," Chasey said, holding up a pink sheet of paper. "I'm supposed to hand out these flyers to people at school."

"Okay." I sighed, holding out my hand.

"I didn't mean you could have one," Chasey laughed. "No offense, but they only gave me a certain number of copies. And if they didn't want you on the panel, well, I guess I should save them."

Argh. Argh. Argh.

"Well," I said. "Hope you get all the opinions you need." All the homogeneous, Chasey-copying, mall-trend-unoriginal opinions you want.

"Come on," Taylor whispered. "Let's just go."

I followed her quickly out the front door. As I was leaving, I held the door for someone else coming in. It turned out to be Arin Morgan in all her gorgeousity, her hands full with a stack of familar pink papers.

"Thanks for holding the door," she said, smiling at me. "And hey, do you go to Independence?"

"Um, yeah," I said. "I'm just a freshman, though."

"Weren't we all freshmen once," Arin said. "It sounds kind of stupid, but I'm on a magazine panel and I'm supposed to pass these flyers out to Independence students."

She held out a flyer to me.

"That's okay," I said. "I don't need one." I don't deserve one, I don't even want one anymore.

"It would really help me out if you would take one," Arin said. "I feel kind of like a loser when people don't even take one from me."

Yeah, right, like Arin Morgan ever felt like a loser. Or like anyone ever said no to her when she smiled like that.

"Oh, fine, I'll take one," I said, taking the sheet of paper.

"Thanks so much," Arin said, smiling at me like I was doing her a huge favor.

I walked past where Taylor was checking her text messages and over to the big trash can on the side of the street. I wanted to get rid of all thoughts and signs of that IT panel. But as the pink paper floated to the top of the trash, the picture on it caught my eye. A picture of something that looked very familiar.

My first thought: Hey, it's my shoe.

My second thought: My shoe looks cute in that photo!

My third thought:

??????????????????????????? !!!!!!!!!!!!!!!!!!!

I'm sorry, but hello? Why is my shoe on the flyer?

I leaned into the trash can and read this:

. . . .

DO YOU KNOW ANYTHING ABOUT THIS SHOE?
The IT panel is looking for the owner of this shoe!
Please contact Whitney at . . .

. . . .

OMG. Omg omg omg.

"Lynn? Why are you sticking your head in the trash can?" Taylor asked. "Are you puking?"

I felt like I was about to. I leaned in farther and grabbed the flyer. I looked at it closer. It was definitely, definitely my shoe in the picture. What the ??????

Taylor came over and looked over my shoulder.

"Lynn! Is that the *GllTter Girl* flyer?" Taylor exclaimed. "Wait a minute, is that your shoe?"

I nodded, speechless.

"Hey! They're looking for you and your shoe!" Taylor exclaimed. "See? It says to call someone named Whitney. You have to call them and tell them that it's your shoe!" She pulled her phone out of the pocket of her backpack.

I shook my head no. My heart was pounding.

"But it's your shoe, Lynn!" Taylor said. "They're look-ing for you!"

"That doesn't mean I want them to find me," I said.

"Think about it. This can't be good. That's a picture of my shoe that flew across the table and knocked Valentyna's food into her lap and probably ruined her priceless outfit. She's probably furious!

"We have to ignore this. We can't tell anyone it's my shoe," I went on, panicked. "Because . . . because everyone would know that it was me being my usual dorky self who basically dumped salad all over a famous fashion designer-slash-editor."

But that wasn't the only reason. I mean, it was not just any famous fashion designer. It was one of my idols.

"Well, okay I guess," Taylor said. "I guess it's your decision. You really don't want to call?"

"Taylor, you're the only one who saw that shoe," I said. "So let's just pretend we never heard about this. Chasey wasn't going to give me a flyer anyway. We'll just rewind to that, okay?"

I threw the flyer back in the garbage can. I still couldn't believe that the shoe I made was plastered on a flyer for everyone at FonDo to see. Then I realized something else. Now tons of people had seen what my shoe looked like. I hoped nobody was laughing at it. Even though nobody would ever know it was mine, it was still out there for all these people to see. What a mess. I'd felt so good about that shoe. . . .

Hopefully it was just Chasey and Arin passing out a few flyers that everyone would toss in the garbage. Hopefully Valentyna would say, Oh well, and get her outfit dry-cleaned. And it would all be over and done. Tra-la-la! Moving on!

I took one last look at the flyer. You could see the detailing on my shoe, like, where I'd drawn that little peace symbol and the teeny little Bella and—I grabbed it back out of the trash can and stuffed the paper in my backpack. My shoe *did* look cute on it. Someday, maybe I'd want to look at it again.

*G*ood morning!" My mother sounded all cheery as she
sat down next to me while I was eating my breakfast.

She was eyeing my outfit but trying not to be too obvious about it. I was getting a lot of attention at home for
my clothes these past few days—for the opposite reason
than I was used to. I was wearing a white polo with a semi-
popped collar. Regular jeans. I'd traded in the seventh-
grade sneakers for another plain white low-top pair that I'd
been planning to embellish with these cool dark red sequins
and—okay, anyway, I left them white. My ponytail was
back for another appearance.

I could tell Mom was torn. She was probably thinking:

A) Yeees! I always wanted a preppy normal-dressing
daughter! And now when I go out in public people won't
look at me like I'm a failure as a mother.

And also:

B) But shouldn't Lynn celebrate her own uniqueness, her own style? Should she feel she has to conform to what everyone else thinks just to "fit in"? And won't I miss seeing what amazingly unique creation she's put together every day?

"Well!" Mom got a big goofy smile on her face. "Let's celebrate the new you! I say we have a mother-daughter day at the mall this weekend to stock up on clothes in your new style!"

Or maybe she was just thinking: A. *Sigh.*

"Orange juice?" Dex said. He put a glass in front of me and poured some. "Can I get you anything else?"

"Uh, Dex? You're not working," I reminded him.

"Oh man!" Dex said. He jumped back. "Geez, I think I'm working too much. I dreamed that I was pouring bubble tea and carrying fondue all night."

I myself dreamed that I was being beaten by a giant shoe. I chose not to share this. I leaned down and gave Bella a piece of my omelet. I wasn't very hungry.

"How is your car fund coming?" my mom asked Dex.

"Tips are okay," Dex said. "But I was thinking about getting another job for the weekends. Is that today's paper? Pass me the part with the Help Wanteds."

I reached over and grabbed the paper. And that's when a pink piece of paper fell out of the newspaper. And on it? A picture of my shoe. It was the same flyer that Chasey and Arin were passing out yesterday. How did it get stuck in our paper?

"Earth to Lynn 2.0. Give me the paper, please?" Dex's

voice was sounding very far away. I shoved the other section toward him.

They were really seriously looking for me if they were stuffing flyers into our paper. Why would they care that much about finding me? Oh no. I must have injured Valentyna. Omigosh, maybe the shoe hit her in the head. Maybe Valentyna was lying in a coma right now in the hospital, and her fashionistas were saying "We must find the evil person who has injured the great Valentyna." Maybe right this second the police were looking for me!

"Lynn?" My mom's voice snapped me out of it. "Your ride is here."

Okay, okay, act normal. Not like a criminal just going off for a regular school day.

"Sounds great, Mom," I croaked. "Okay! Bye!"

I grabbed the newspaper and bolted out the door.

"Hello, Lynn!" Mrs. Snyder said as I climbed into the car. "Well! Don't you look nice today."

"Thank you, Mrs. Snyder," I said. "Backseat," I whispered to Taylor, who was sitting in the second row. She jumped into the way-back with me.

"What's up?" Taylor asked.

"I have to talk to you *privately*," I whispered, and pointed to her mother. Taylor's mother liked to listen in to our conversations. She told Taylor it helped her "stay young." Taylor told me she was just nosy.

Taylor took out her cell phone and dialed. Suddenly, her mom's cell phone rang.

"Oh! My phone! Now where's that thing?" her mother

asked herself, driving and trying to find her phone in her giant gold handbag.

"She's distracted," Taylor whispered. "What's up?"

"Taylor, I'm in trouble," I said, holding up the paper. "Look what was in the morning newspaper."

"Hey!" Taylor said. "That's your shoe!"

"There's a manhunt," I said. "I must have injured Valentyna or something. They're looking for me, Taylor."

"Oh no, what are you going to do?" Taylor said.

"I don't know."

"Well, they didn't say Valentyna was seriously injured or anything," Taylor mused. "They would have said that on the news, right? Maybe she's not hurt. Maybe she's just mad about it and trying to track you down for revenge or something."

"Aw crud, I better turn myself in," I said. "This can't go any further."

"Do you want to use my phone to call them?" Taylor asked, handing her cell to me.

I took a deep breath and dialed the number.

"Thanks for calling *GlITter Girl* magazine," a voice answered.

"You're welcome. I mean—I'm calling about the shoe," I stammered.

"Is this the media?" the voice asked. "For media inquiries, please press nine."

"Um, no, actually I'm the person who made the shoe," I said.

"Yes, we've heard that from quite a few people today,"

the voice said. "Before you continue, know that Valentyna is not meeting with people personally. She's in Paris."

"Okay, phew, so she's not injured or in the hospital or anything?" I interrupted. That was a relief.

"Excuse me? Valentyna is fine and fabulous as usual," she said. "What we need you to do is e-mail us a photo of you with the other shoe."

"The other shoe?" I said.

"Yes," she said. "Shoes come in pairs? We need our shoe owner to show us the match for proof of ownership."

"I totally would, but I threw it in the trash."

And she laughed.

"Well, that's an excuse I haven't heard yet! You threw the other shoe in the trash," she said. "Hon, how old are you?"

"I'm a freshman in high school," I said.

"In a few years you'll be old enough for our fashion internship," she said. "Apply then and who knows, maybe you can break into fashion and even meet Valentyna someday. I give all of you people calling here credit for having the gumption to pretend to have made the shoe, just to try to come in."

"What? What're they saying?" Taylor whispered.

"She doesn't believe it's my shoe," I said, covering the phone. "She thinks I'm just trying to meet Valentyna or crash their office or something."

Hey. That was *my* shoe. Nobody else better be claiming my shoe. I felt slightly offended.

"Um, seriously," I said, "I made that shoe. I mean, I know everyone at school thinks I'm, like, this freak for wearing stuff like that, and throwing the other shoe in the trash was kind of stupid I guess, but—"

"Another call is coming in!" the woman said. "Well, please feel free to e-mail Valentyna through our website. Valentyna reads all of her fan mail, but of course she doesn't have time to respond individually."

And she hung up.

"She didn't believe me," I said. I had mixed emotions. On one hand, I'd tried to turn myself in so I wouldn't feel guilty anymore. On the other hand, people were claiming they'd made my shoe, and I'd poured my heart into that shoe. Still, that shoe had ended up in Valentyna's salad . . . so maybe this was for the best. I'd stay anonymous and the whole thing would blow over.

"Wait, what are you going to do?" Taylor asked me. "You can't just let it go!"

"That's exactly what I'm doing," I said calmly as we pulled up to school. "I called and now it's done. We move on. I go back to being a normal, invisible nobody at school."

I looked down at my boring white Converse sneaks. Yes, that was my future. A very normal, invisible nobody.

11

W hat is the answer to problem nine? Let's hear from Vincent Lynn," Mr. Lowe called out.

It took me a moment to realize I was being called on. Just call me Vinnie. I was in math, my last class. I had been very effective at being normal and invisible all day, and I didn't want to ruin my perfect record. I opened my mouth to give the answer when the class TV monitor suddenly flashed on, interrupting me.

"I'm Fletcher from Independence High News Network, with our end of the day live news report." The guy smiled into the camera.

"Is this necessary in the middle of my class?" Mr. Lowe grumbled.

Necessary no, but welcome, yes. Since I was off the hook for a minute. I double-checked my answer.

"Woot! Hot chicks on TV!" some guy's voice called out.

"And for a special report, I'm here with Arin Morgan and Chasey Welch," the TV guy was saying.

I looked up from my math notebook.

"We're on this *GlITter Girl* magazine IT panel," Chasey was saying. "And tons of girls tried out for it, but the only two people from our school selected were me and Arin."

Don't hold back, Chasey.

"We're here because a fashion designer, Valentyna, asked the panelists for help finding the owner of a shoe," Arin said.

Oh no.

"What happened was someone lost a shoe at the teen IT panel auditions at the mall," Chasey explained. "So all the panelists have been asked to put the word out to their schools."

"What's so special about a shoe?" the reporter asked.

Aw, jeez. Here we go. Okay, I tripped! I tripped and my shoe flew off!! And yes, it hit Valentyna! I was sorry! It was an accident! An innocent mistake! A mistake that was being broadcast across our school TV news!

I flopped my head back down on my desk.

"There *is* something special about this shoe," Arin said. "It's so hard to explain to anyone who hasn't seen the shoe in real life. But it's such an epic shoe. Valentyna wants to know where the teen bought the shoe so she can find out who designed it."

Um, huh? I lifted my head up.

"It's so exciting, it's like a Cinderella story," Arin said.

A picture of my shoe flashed on the screen.

"Cool shoe," the girl behind me said.

Did that girl just say my shoe was cool?

"So if anyone knows anything about this shoe, please contact—"

"This is nonsense, interrupting my lesson for this," Mr. Lowe announced and turned off the TV. "Back to business. Vincent Lynn, what is number nine?"

And thankfully, the bell rang and saved me. My head was whirling as I tried to escape before my luck changed. I walked out the door in a blur and headed down to my locker, where I promptly stuck my head in and inhaled the scent of the flower air freshener thingy. I needed a break to quietly gather my thoughts about all of this.

"I think there's a girl stuck in that locker," a voice said nearby.

I quickly pulled my head out of my locker and looked up to see Jacob at his locker—with Chasey.

"Hey, Lynn," Jacob said. "Do you know Chasey?"

"Yes," I said at the same time Chasey said, "No."

Jacob looked confused. Chasey leaned on Jacob's locker so her back was facing me.

"So did you see me on the news?" Chasey asked Jacob.

I shuffled my books around in my locker. Not that I was eavesdropping or anything but okay, I was.

"Yeah, that was pretty cool," Jacob said.

"Thanks," Chasey said. "I'm thinking of getting an agent."

"No, I meant it was cool about the shoe mystery," Jacob said. "Don't you think so, Lynn?"

"Um, yeah, huh?" I said. "Sorry, were you talking?"

"Did you see that story about the shoe on the school news?" Jacob asked.

"Jacob," Chasey said, cutting him off. "Shh. Lynn actually tried out for the IT panel and didn't make it. We don't want to make her feel bad."

"I didn't mean to," Jacob said. "It's just that I thought of you when I saw the shoe. It looked like something you would wear. Or you used to wear."

I looked down at my outfit. A peach T-shirt I'd originally bought so I could thread it with teeny ribbons and repurpose it into a skirt. Jeans I'd thrifted that I'd been planning to bleach and—

"You thought of *Lynn?*" Chasey said scornfully, but then caught the look on Jacob's face and backtracked. "It's just that, it's like this *designer* shoe, probably really expensive from Europe that this famous designer said she loved."

"Chasey?" I seized the moment. "What exactly *did* Valentyna say about the shoe?"

"She said that the shoe was unique, fresh, and so of-the-moment. When the IT panel finds out who made the shoe, I'll be the first to wear them."

The bell rang and I jumped.

"I gotta run," Jacob said, waving to me as Chasey followed him. "Later, Lynn."

At that point, I basically collapsed against the locker. Processing, processing. I let it sink in what Chasey said:

Valentyna thought my shoe was unique, fresh, and of-the-moment? Slowly, a grin spread across my face.

"Ooooh." Someone came up behind me and made me jump again. It was Taylor. "I know why you're smiling!" she cooed.

"You do?" I asked.

"You were flirting with Jacob Elias!" she said.

"I wasn't flirting," I protested. "You won't believe what Chasey just said about my shoe."

"I will believe it," Taylor interrupted. "But right now, no more talking, just hurry. I'll give you something to really smile about. My mom's giving you a ride home. And I've got a surprise for you."

Taylor leaned back against the seat of her mom's car and hit the button on her cell phone to replay the video.

"We're here at the *GlITter Girl* IT panel audition," Taylor's voice said. "Check out Lynn's shoe. It rocks!"

"I do love my shoe!" I heard myself say.

I watched on-screen as Taylor and I put our arms around each other and I held up the shoe.

"You said you deleted that from your phone!" I said. "You promised!"

"I swear I did!" Taylor said. "But I forgot that when I take a video I e-mail it to myself! I went into my sent box and ta-da! There was a copy!"

Taylor looked triumphant.

"So, duh, I called *GlITter Girl* back and e-mailed them the video," Taylor said. "And now, we have an appointment to iChat on my laptop with them in ten minutes."

I sank back in the car seat. This was slightly overwhelming.

"I'm nauseous," I said. "I think I'm going to throw up."

"Why?" Taylor said. "Remember when they didn't believe you this morning? Now you get to tell *GlITter Girl* the shoe is yours!"

"They're looking for a shoe designer, for someone cool," I told her. "And look what they're getting. A klutzy high school nobody. I'm going to be a total disappointment. An embarrassment to their search."

"You *are* someone cool," Taylor said.

Awwww . . . that was sweet.

"You won't be a total disappointment," Taylor said.

Awww . . .

"You could never be an embarrassment," Taylor continued. "No wait, yes you could. Remember when you bleached those jeans and didn't wash off the bleach enough? And when you wore them, everyone in class was like: What is that smell?"

Taylor cracked up.

"Oh, and remember when you brought that pillow you made to a sleepover, but the fabric glue was still wet and when you lay down it stuck to your head?" Taylor laughed. "We had to cut your hair."

She was really laughing now.

"Um, hello?" I said. "I thought we were supposed to be boosting my confidence here?" Then I remembered something. "Oh wait, remember when I tie-dyed a baseball hat and it wasn't dry yet and it turned my hair green?"

Even I couldn't help myself. I started cracking up, too.

"We're here, girls," Taylor's mother called out. "Tay-Tay, I will pick you up at five for your back handspring prep class."

"Thanks for the ride, Mrs. Snyder," I said loudly, covering up Taylor's groan.

I hit the garage code, and we went inside my house.

"I'll sign on," Taylor said, opening her laptop at my kitchen table.

"I'm really nervous," I said to her. "Are you sure I should do this?"

"Yup," Taylor said. "I'm positive."

I stared at the laptop screen as Taylor pulled up the webcam.

"I'm not getting a good wireless signal." Taylor frowned. She picked up the computer and carried it through the kitchen, then upstairs.

"Try my room," I suggested. "It's closer to my brother's wireless base."

We ended up in my closet, where the wireless was working best. I worked up my nerve for what was going to happen next.

"They're accepting our chat!" Taylor said, and pointed to the words "*GlITter Girl* accepts" on the screen. A video screen popped up and a woman's face peered at us.

"Hi! I'm Taylor, just the friend," Taylor said, and

pointed at me. "This is who you're looking for. Lynn!"

"Hi, girls, I'm Whitney," she said. Whitney had very curly brown hair on top of which she wore a cute patterned headband. "I'm Valentyna's personal assistant. We've had a lot of calls from people who claim they designed the shoe. I'm sure you realize many people believe this is an opportunity for some visibility in the field of fashion."

We nodded.

"So when we got the video you e-mailed, we were quite excited," Whitney said. "But still, I'd like to clear your story before we tell Valentyna. Lynn?"

"Well, I made the shoe," I said. "And I just really wanted to say I'm sorry for the whole disaster when I lost it."

"Can you tell me more about that?" Whitney asked.

"Well, I was wearing the shoe when Taylor and I went to the *GlITter Girl* IT panel audition at Independence Mall," I said.

"We didn't see your name or Taylor's name on the audition list," Whitney said.

"It's kind of a long story, but I didn't get in to audition," I said.

"Where's the other shoe?" Whitney asked. "Do you have the match?"

"I threw it out," I said. "I was kind of upset about not auditioning, so we went to this deli and then I saw Valentyna in one of the booths. I wanted a closer look at her, but I tripped, and my shoe flew into her salad. Can you please tell her I'm so sorry about that? I feel so stupid. I ruined her sweater, and I think I knocked over the plate of corned beef she ordered for Pasha and—"

"Kindly excuse me for one moment," Whitney said, and she paused the screen. The iChat went dark.

"What just happened?" Taylor whispered.

I didn't know. We waited. And then the video filled the screen again. But this time, it wasn't Whitney's face.

It was Valentyna. I gasped.

"Hello, ladies," Valentyna said. She had her black hair pulled back in a signature scarf, yellow and silver.

"I think I'll leave you two alone," Taylor said, getting up, and walking out of the closet before I could stop her.

"Lynn," Valentyna said, in the booming yet gentle voice I'd heard on the Style Network. "Lynn, Lynn, Lynn. So *you* made the shoe."

"Honest, I swear I made the shoe," I babbled. "And I'm so so sorry. I should have stayed and apologized for ruining your lunch but I panicked and—"

"No apologies are necessary," Valentyna laughed. "It was a rather unusual moment, but a fortuitous one. Imagine my surprise when I discovered, sitting on my salad plate, a fabulously original, creative, and unique shoe."

Oh! The stupid grin crept across my face again.

"Lynn, can you tell me about your shoe?" Valentyna continued.

"Well," I said. "I made it to wear to the IT panel audition."

"Lynn." Valentyna leaned in and looked me straight in

the eye. *"Really* tell me about your shoe. Tell me about when you were making it. What inspired the shoe?"

I took a deep breath. I looked around my closet and remembered that moment when I was here, in this exact location, about to make the shoe.

Then I told Valentyna everything. How I created clothes and things that I thought were totally me. How I was always known as the girl who wore weird clothes. How it seemed natural to me to express myself through my creations, but nobody but me seemed to understand that. And how I'd been hoping maybe in high school I'd find someone else like me or at least that I'd be more accepted. But instead I was still the weird girl.

But I also told her about Taylor and Grace and how they didn't exactly understand but they also didn't mind what I wore. And how the stuff I made didn't always work out, like when my sock unraveled and got stuck but how Jacob rescued me. And of course, what inspired me to make the shoe.

I leaned back in my chair, exhausted from blabbing. Valentyna hadn't said a word. She just looked at me.

"Lynn, do you know what I'm thinking right now?" Valentyna asked.

"Um, maybe why are you stuck on video chat with a babbling freak?" I said.

Valentyna laughed.

"Not quite," she said. "I was thinking you've confirmed some of my thoughts about the shoe. When I saw the shoe, I knew there was a story behind it. It was exquisitely fresh and new. It also was weakly constructed and obviously made by an amateur—"

"I know, I'm so embarrassed," I blurted out. "One of the pictures fell off, I need to use a different glue maybe or—"

"Lynn!" Valentyna interrupted. "That's not what I meant. In fact, all of that added to its appeal, because I knew the shoe was created by someone who was untrained and untainted. The shoe spoke to me. And—wait a minute. Is that shirt behind you one of the photographs you used on the shoe? Did you make that?"

I turned around to see the black T-shirt into which I'd sewn a wide pink ribbon across the neckline. I'd threaded a smaller ribbon through one of the sides and tied it into a bow and slashed the bottom of it, for a girly-meets-rocker look.

"Yes," I said. "All the pictures are of outfits and things I made."

"Those pictures aren't from clip art or someone else's work?" she asked.

"No!" I said. "I made all the clothes, and added things I love, like my dog and my friends. I know, I wear weird clothes."

"Lynn," Valentyna said. "You say you wear what you call weird clothes. What are you wearing right now?"

I looked down. I was wearing the old T-shirt, jeans, and white sneaks deal.

"Oh. Well, after the IT panel disaster I kind of, well, gave up," I admitted. "I decided to dress like everyone else and blend in."

"Ah," Valentyna said. "Well, what did you wear before the blending? Say, on the first day of school?"

"I have a picture of it, right here," I said. I brought the laptop over for a close-up on the Wall of LynnSpiration.

"Nice collage," Valentyna asked. "Now the outfit next to it? That doesn't seem to fit . . . ?"

"Oh, that's the outfit I put together for Taylor," I said. "She didn't know what to wear the first day of school."

"So you put outfits together for others, too?" Valentyna nodded.

I described all my creations . . . the shirts, jeans, sweaters, hats, the flute cover, the backpacks. I told her the story behind each of the outfits. I forgot where I was and who I was talking to. I just talked.

And when a ring tone went off, we both jumped.

"That's my phone," Valentyna said, checking it.

"I'm sorry," I apologized. "I didn't mean to talk like that forever. I know you have other things to do."

"Please don't apologize," Valentyna said. "I've thoroughly enjoyed our chat. And now, I'd like to offer you an opportunity. I know you didn't have the chance to audition for the IT panel . . ."

"You're letting me audition to be on the IT panel?" I exclaimed. "I get a second chance? That's awesome!"

"Lynn, you're misunderstanding," Valentyna laughed. "I'm not offering you the opportunity to audition for the IT panel. I'm not even offering you the opportunity to *be* on the IT panel."

"Oh, sure," I said, embarrassed. "That was stupid of me to think you'd want me for—"

"Lynn!" Valentyna stopped me. She got up from her chair and leaned over her desk toward me. "I don't want you for the IT panel, I want you to be IT."

Now I was totally lost.

"As you know, *GlITter Girl* put together the IT panel to help with ideas for their online magazine," Valentyna said. "And the girls on the panel are excellent choices. They're the girls who first notice trends and wear them. Girls that others think are in the know, who are looked up to in different ways."

Like Arin and Chasey.

"But you are different." Valentyna moved closer to the computer screen. "You've created something yourself, with your own unique way of expressing yourself. And when I saw your shoe, something spoke to me. You made this shoe to represent the *real* you. Not what your peers or society or even our magazine wants you to be, is that correct to say?"

I nodded, speechless.

"This shoe is a statement of a true *GlITter Girl* IT Girl," Valentyna said. "I made a suggestion to *GlITter Girl* that they are happy to implement. I suggested that your shoe should be featured on their new website. Is that appealing to you?"

I opened my mouth. Nothing came out.

"I'm taking that as a yes." Valentyna smiled.

My mother agreed. Valentyna had my mom call her at her office and then shared the whole story. Then Valentyna had asked to speak with me one more time.

"And tomorrow? Please do not wear an outfit like that," she said, smiling. "It is all wrong."

I knew exactly what she meant. All the feelings I'd had when I was making the shoe flooded back to me. I was ready to be *me* again.

So today I went back to dressing as me. I wore: patchwork cropped pants I'd made from pieces of T-shirts and uniforms from the sports I'd tried (and failed embrarrassingly at) . . . soccer, softball, peewee cheerleading . . . but now they were finally being put to good use! My mom's old black blazer I'd slashed up a bit, with a white tee underneath. A big bow on the side of my head. It would have been perfect with The Shoes, but of course one was probably in a garbage landfill somewhere and the other was with Valentyna. Waiting to have its picture taken to be on *GllTter Girl Online*!!!!!!

Instead, I put on thrifted clunky black boots. Yeah, people had stared at me all day in school again. Yeah, people were giving me weird looks now at FonDo. But I was still Happy and In Shock as I sat at our table in the back of FonDo, listening to Taylor tell Grace the whole story.

"So that's what happened," Taylor finished. "Can you believe it?"

Grace looked back and forth at me and Taylor.

"So, let me get this straight," she said. "Lynn, the Lynn sitting here right in front of me, designed that shoe. And now your shoe is going to be on the *GllTter Girl* magazine website?"

"Yessss!" squealed Taylor. "I knew we all needed to celebrate. But you can't tell anyone, Grace. It's a secret until Lynn gives us the word."

"So what happens next?" Grace asked.

"I really don't know too much," I said. "Except that the site is going up soon."

"Well, congratulations," Grace said, and held up her water glass. We clinked our glasses together.

"Are you celebrating? Did someone win the Loser of the Year award?" someone said. Ugh. Chasey was walking back. Kayden was right behind her.

We all froze for a second. Then I remembered what we were celebrating and I relaxed.

"Aw, Lynn is back to wearing her Freak clothes today.

You couldn't handle being normal for more than a couple days?" Chasey asked me.

"I like Lynn's outfit," Taylor said.

"That's why *you're* back here sitting with her, and *I'm* sitting in the front," Chasey said.

"I thought my outfit was kind of *GlITter Girl*–inspired," I said innocently.

"She's delusional," Chasey said. "Lynn, you didn't make the IT panel. Move on with your life."

I tried not to meet Taylor's and Grace's eyes.

"Wait, you guys, I'm getting a text message from *GlITter Girl*," Chasey said, looking at her phone. "No way! They found the person who made The Shoe!"

"They found the person?" Kayden squealed. "Does it say who?"

No, it wouldn't. They were keeping me secret.

"Oh yeah, they told her name," Chasey said importantly. "But it's confidential for the IT panel."

Now I really couldn't look at Taylor and Grace or I'd burst out laughing.

"Can't you tell *me*?" Kayden asked.

"Nopee," Chasey said cheerfully. "I'm the only one here who can know."

"Too bad you didn't make the IT panel," I said slyly to Kayden.

"Kayden understands that they wanted the ultimate alpha trendsetters and well, Kayden is still learning from me, right?" Chasey said. "But I share the glory. Like I gave

Kayden the T-shirt they gave us in a goodie bag. It was too big for me, anyway."

Kayden frowned.

"Do you guys want to sit down?" I asked them. "Obviously you want to hang out with us so—"

"What? No, we were just going to the girls' room," Chasey said. "We're not hanging out."

I didn't look up until they were gone. And then I lost it. I started laughing, and all three of us just cracked up.

"I love when she said, 'Move on with your life,'" Taylor laughed. "Omigosh, I almost lost it right there."

"Only I, the exclusively exclusive *GlITter Girl* IT panel member, know the secret identity." Grace did a surprisingly killer imitation of Chasey.

"And none of you little people can know," I said, continuing the imitation. "That includes you, Kayden, my supposed BFF."

"Chasey is going to die when she finds out it's Lynn," Taylor said, practically hysterical.

"You mean Liz," I corrected her.

"Ouch, my cheeks hurt," Grace said. "I'm laughing too hard."

I'd been stressed, worried, and in general freaked about everything that had happened. But right now, it was all good.

"You guys!" Grace whispered. "People are looking at us!"

I looked up. She was right. And I smiled. Let them.

I sat on my bedroom floor with my newest thrifted find. I wasn't sure what it was going to be yet, but it was this black boa with enormous feathers. I went over to my mirror and held it up. I put it under my arm . . . no, not a bag. But it was too much for a shirt, even for me. Around my waist? On my head? I giggled and tossed it around my neck.

"Hello," I said into the mirror. "I am the IT Girl. Aren't I glamorous?"

"No, you're strange."

I whipped around. Dex was standing in my doorway.

"I should have filmed it with my cell," Dex said. "IT Girl wearing weird fluffy thing talks to herself in the mirror."

"Don't even go there. You *sing* to your bathroom mirror." I started singing. "Oh Arrrin, if you only kneeewww! You're the girl for me!"

"Dang, you can hear that?" Dex said. He looked flustered. "Truce."

"Truce," I agreed.

"Mom called. She's going to be late tonight," Dex said, putting his blue laundry basket on my bed. "I'm supposed to make dinner and you're on laundry duty, so here. Oh, and she told me about your shoe thing."

"Yeah," I said. "How weird is that?"

"Freakishly," Dex said. "I mean, you? No offense, but— you?"

"I'd be offended but honestly, I'm thinking the same thing," I said. "After being made fun of all my life for my clothes and stuff, all of a sudden something I made is going to be in a fashion magazine? Totally insane."

"Well, you're talented," Dex said. "So I guess it's not *that* insane."

"Did you just call me talented?" I asked. I pretended to look around. "Me? Your sister?"

"Obviously you're talented," Dex said. "I just figured you and I would be unappreciated for our talents in high school and then our genius would be recognized later in life. Like I'll be a Bill Gates someday and you'd win *Project Runway* season twenty or something. I guess your genius is getting appreciated first."

"Thanks," I said, touched. "Don't worry, your genius will be appreciated someday, too. Until then, you can be one of my fashion models if you want."

"Yeah, that's me," Dex said, flexing. "I think chicken legs and bony arms are going to be hot on the runway this season, don't you? Anyway, congrats on the shoe thing."

Dex left and I sighed as I picked up his basket of laundry. I saw a plain gray long-sleeved polo shirt on top. I pulled out the shirt and went to my closet and got to work. A half hour later, I admired my work. I'd cut the sleeves to three-quarter length, and added a little stitched *D*. I replaced the buttons with computer chips for a high-tech look. And then I took the leftover gray material and made a cell phone cover. When I was finished, I held it up and smiled. It wasn't much, but I hope he liked it. I went to Dex's room and knocked on the door.

"What?" he asked.

"You said you wanted to be my model, right?" I held up the shirt. "If you wear it untucked and don't pull your pants up so high, I bet even Arin Morgan will think you look, well, almost cool in this."

I sat down at one of the computers in study hall. First, I checked Style.com for my daily fix. Then I went to my e-mail. Spam, spam, and what was this from *GlITter Girl?*

Lynn, please click on the link for a sneak preview of your shoe online. Please let us know if you have any issues before the site goes live.

Whitney, *GlITter Girl Online* editor

I gasped so loudly people turned to look at me. But really, this was huge. I was about to get a sneak preview of my shoe's debut. Oh, I hoped it looked okay. I took a deep breath and clicked on the link. A silver screen that glittered came up, with fuchsia writing:

. . . .

GLITTER GIRL Online
Up-to-the-minute
Fashion, style,
and
inside information . . .
Exclusive styles like . . . THE SHOE

. . . .

And then suddenly, something spun on to the screen. A giant picture of my shoe. I gasped when I realized my shoe was the home page. I mean, I knew the shoe would be on there, but I thought it would be some extra feature you'd find after clicking around for a while. I couldn't stop smiling as I stared at each of the collaged pictures on it. I clicked on Bella's cute little pug face, and how cool was this?—it enlarged for a close-up view. It was like my Wall of Lynn-Spiration had come to life.

This was very, very cool. I clicked on an arrow, and the shoe rotated so you could see the other side in a 360-degree view. They'd put back in the picture of Taylor and me hugging, though it was fuzzy. Well, they probably didn't want to have my face on the website. And that was okay by me; it was cool enough that my shoe was there. Anytime I wanted to see it, I could just pull up this website. And pretty soon, anytime anyone would want to see it, they could pull up the website, too.

The caption said:

The Shoe—
Designed by a teen . . .
discovered by fashion icon Valentyna.

. . . .

That was me! I'm the teen! I felt a little bit famous, even though of course I was totally anonymous. I felt so proud of my shoe. I felt pure joy.

Then I noticed a button at the bottom of the page.

. . . .

ONLINE POLLS!
GlITter Girl magazine wants YOUR opinion!
What do you think of our new website?
What do you want to see in the future?
What do you think of The Shoe?
Rate The Shoe from 1 to 5 stars.

. . . .

Yeeps. Add nervousness to my pure joy. I guess I was only glad I was going to be anonymous. People were going to rate my shoe? What if they were going to rate it a 1 or a 2 or a zero? What if they thought it was ugly and they'd never go to GlITter Girl Online again? This was way, way too much pressure.

I wondered if the poll was working. The website wasn't live yet, but wait. I wasn't the only one who was getting a sneak preview. I saw at the bottom there were thirty-four users online at that very moment. Other people were sneaking previews, maybe fashion people, or wait, probably the IT panel. Yikes, right now the IT panel could be staring at my shoe and voting in the poll. Maybe I should rate my own shoe. Was that cheating? I poised the mouse over the rating 5 stars. Wait, maybe that was too obvious, maybe I should rate it a 4. But what if I was the only one rating it? I should just go for it and make it look good. I clicked the 5 stars. The vote was loading when I realized I'd be able to see the poll results. What were the results? Did I even want to know?

"Excuse me, but it's my turn to use this computer," a girl's voice behind me said. I turned around to see a girl in a cheerleading uniform standing behind me.

"Can you wait just a second?" I asked her, silently urging the poll to hurry up and load.

"No, I've got to print a paper like *now*," the girl said.

Alrighty, thanks for your good cheer, cheerleader. I sighed and logged off the computer. I could see the reflection of the cheerleader as she pulled at her turtleneck.

"Sorry," she said behind me. "I didn't mean to sound obnoxious. This uniform is so freaking uncomfortable it puts me in a bad mood by the end of the day."

"That's okay," I said. "I know what you mean. These lace sleeves seemed like a good idea at the time, but they're kind of itchy."

"At least they're cute," she said. "Unlike our uniforms, which not only choke me but are ugly."

I stood up to give her the seat at the computer and smiled at her in sympathy. I went to the sign-in sheet to try to get another computer, but they were taken. Crud.

I sat at a free desk behind my former computer carrel. I noticed the cheerleader looked seriously uncomfortable as she pulled at her turtleneck. I don't know who picked out those cheer uniforms, but not only did they look itchy, they were also seriously not flattering. I didn't blame her for being cranky. They would look much better if they didn't have the turtleneck and had a rounder neckline instead. And the skirts could be so much cuter if they didn't have that weird pleat. . . . I started to sketch. I drew a few different styles until I did one I liked.

I went over to the cheerleader, still at the computer, scratching her neck. I ripped out a sheet of paper from my notebook and slid it onto her keyboard.

And as I was heading back to the desk, I looked up and saw my brother passing the doorway. He was wearing the shirt I'd made for him, and even I had to admit he was looking pretty good. Since I had to take my mind off my shoe poll, I might as well think of something else for him. I turned to a fresh page in my notebook and started to sketch.

I slid off my sneakers as I entered the house after school. I had drawn stars all over them with my silver marker on the bus ride home, obviously due to the fact that I was anxious about the shoe poll. It had been a few days where things seemed to quiet down and be somewhat normal. Other than the fact that I kept checking on my shoe poll to see if any results had been posted.

"And Lynn just came home," she said into the phone, and then held the phone out to me. "It's Valentyna."

"Hello?" I said, taking the phone.

"Lynn, I just found out something that I found disturbing," Valentyna said.

"Oh no," I said, and went to sit down on the stairs. It must be the poll. I must have gotten zero stars, and Valentyna realized that she'd made a huge mistake thinking my shoe was cool and now they were pulling it off the site.

"There was a poll about your shoe on the *GlITter Girl* site," Valentyna said.

"I know," I sighed.

"You know?" Valentyna said. "Oh dear, I wanted to intercept you first. I'm so disappointed that you would have to face that."

"Oh jeesh, how bad were the poll results?" I winced.

"The results?" Valentyna asked. "Oh, they were fabulous, of course. Five stars almost unanimously. But the point is—"

"Five stars? People liked my shoe?" I asked her.

"Of course they liked it," Valentyna said. "I told you it was fabulous. I'm just disturbed that *GlITter Girl* would host a poll about the shoe without telling you in advance. To me, fashion is subjective, and to quantify it into numbers saps the creativity and individuality."

"I can see your point," I said. But I was thinking, *Girls liked my shoe!* My mind was racing. It was all hitting me. Usually people saw my creations on me, like at school or something. Then they wouldn't see my creations, they'd just be judging me. So this was the first time my creation was judged . . . for itself. It had nothing to do with me. It was totally anonymous. And girls loved it! OTHER PEOPLE LOVED MY SHOE!

I heard the call waiting beep on our phone. Caller ID said GLITTER GIRL.

"Oh, it's *GlITter Girl* calling," I blurted out, thrown off guard.

"Go ahead and take that, my dear," Valentyna said.

"And feel free to let them know if you're as disappointed as I am about the polling situation."

"Thank you, Valentyna," I said, and clicked back over to say hello.

"Lynn? It's Whitney from *GlITter Girl*. I have fabulous, and I mean fabulous news. Did you see the website poll? I wanted to tell you our results. Nearly eighty-nine point seven percent of our preview trendsetters voted your shoe five stars, and six percent voted four stars. Lynn, that shoe is absolutely vanguard."

Um, I think that's a good thing.

"Valentyna told us about the conversation she had with you and I had a flash of brilliance! It's the perfect story arc. Unappreciated outcast's wish comes true with her DIY fashion skills. So we need to jump on this for the launch while we're striking our demographic."

"I'm not really following you," I confessed.

"You're resonating with our demographic—that is, our audience. Teen fashionista trendsetters are picky customers, Lynn. If they love you, we want more of you. As Valentyna said, you need to be our very first IT Girl. We'll do a story on you and how the shoe was created and discovered."

"You'll do a story about me?" I stammered.

"You'll be the very first face of *GlITter Girl Online*. We will introduce you to the world as one of our own discoveries. A real teen with her own sense of style. Your mother offered to take a photo of you tonight and send it to us ASAP so we can get started. That's the beauty of the website. We can post the hot news as it happens! Just wear an outfit that completely expresses you and complements the shoe. I told your mom we want to see your complete style. Now, I have to take another call. You're a doll."

And she hung up. I stood there with the phone in my hand, and my head was spinning.

I stared at the phone. Emotional roller coaster was back. People liked my shoe! They rated it ★★★★★!

★★★★★! Out of ★★★★★!

And *GlITter Girl* wants *me* to be on the website! Not just my shoe, *me*. Was this a good thing? Could I really put myself out there? Yes! Of course I could! This was my moment! And wait a minute!

I looked in the mirror as I realized something. They wanted a picture of me tonight? But wait. I should get a haircut. And a makeover! These late nights were giving me bags under my eyes. And I had a zit. Wait a minute, I'm not ready for this. I changed my mind.

I picked up the phone to call Whitney back. Then I put it back down. I couldn't miss this opportunity because of a zit. Silly me. I'd just put on concealer and get dressed and—ack! What was I going to wear? I needed to find an outfit that would be cool enough for the designer of the shoe. Full-on panic set in. I flopped facedown onto my bed. The emotional roller coaster was about to crash.

"Mooom!" I yelled. "Moooom?"

"Are you off the phone?" My mother came in. "This is very exciting. Honey? You don't look excited."

"This!" I pointed to myself. "I'm supposed to be the Face of the website launch? I'm not the Face of anything, except the Face of Someone who needs pimple cream."

"Lynn, you always look wonderful."

"You're my mother, you have to say that," I pointed out.

"And how you look is not what's important," my mom said. "I'm happy to see this magazine is placing value on creativity, imagination, uniqueness. They want their readers to see who's behind the shoe. And that's you."

"Well, they're all obviously going to be disappointed," I grumbled. "Possibly horrified."

"Anyway, I promised them a photo tonight," Mom said, smiling. "So pull yourself together. No worries."

"No worries? This is going to be in an online *fashion* magazine. That's huge worries. What should I wear?" I wailed.

"I'm going to get my camera," my mom said cheerfully, "while you hit your closet."

I slid off my bed and went into my closet. And I had thought the pressure of the first day of school was bad. I stood paralyzed at the door of my closet and felt totally overwhelmed. What should I wear? I backed away from my closet and flopped on my bed. Ouch, I landed on my phone. I picked it up . . . and dialed Taylor.

"*You're* calling *me* for clothes advice?" Taylor replied when I told her. "Who is this? Am I being punked?"

"Stop it," I said. "It's just *GlITter Girl* wants a picture of me and my mother has to take it tonight and I'm freaking out."

"You? Freak out over what to wear?" Taylor said. "You're the maestro of clothes."

"Taylor! Just . . . augh!" I let out a wail.

"Okay, okay, don't panic," Taylor said. "Don't move. We'll be there in ten minutes."

She hung up. We? I hoped she meant to say *I*. I didn't want anyone else to see me in this condition.

I wrapped some purple satiny material around my head, strategically covering the pimple. Maybe I could kick off the forehead wrap as a fashion statement. Yes, girls with zit-foreheads everywhere would be grateful to me for this new and practical fashion.

I checked myself out in the mirror and uhhh . . . no. Not only did it look ridiculous, it screamed Lame Attempt to cover a zit. I hoped they would at least airbrush my zit out. Better yet, maybe they could airbrush my whole face. Hmm, maybe I should just drape the material over my face completely.

"Knock knock!" I heard Taylor's voice at the door.

"Come in," I said. The door opened. And in walked Taylor. And . . . Grace?

"I hope you don't mind I brought Grace," Taylor said.

"She was at my house studying for our wellness test. And then when you called, well . . ."

"I hope it's okay," Grace said, and looked down at her light brown T-shirt and khaki cargo pants. "Not that I think I'll be any help with clothes advice, but maybe I can give moral support."

"Thanks you, guys," I said. That was nice of her, but also kind of humiliating. It was pretty awkward. "I feel really stupid about this."

"Oh, puh-lease!" Taylor said. "About asking for help? That's what friends are for. The only thing you should feel stupid about is, well, that thing unraveling around your head."

Oh yeah. I forgot about the zit-cover. I felt it. It was unwrapping and starting to hang over my eye.

"I have a huge pimple," I confessed.

"No problemo!" Taylor said. She opened up her backpack and took out a giant pink fluffy case. "You sounded like you needed to de-stress, so I brought my spa kit. We can give you a facial."

Taylor steered me over to a chair. Before I could even process what was going on, she pushed my hair back with my headband and started putting a green mud mask on my face.

"I can do your nails. I'm pretty good at it," Grace assured me. "I give myself a manicure all the time, since I have to stare at my fingers playing the piano."

I picked bright pink and lay back. Taylor gooped my

face and gave me a little neck massage. Grace painted my nails. I started to relax a little bit and zone out.

"It's pretty amazing that you'll be representing all of us," Taylor suddenly said. "Not just our school, your friends, but you are representing all of the little people who aren't supermodels and IT panel–type people."

The stress was back.

"That's why I feel so much pressure," I said. "What if everyone looks at my picture and is like, *she* made the shoe? And what if they're all disappointed? And if that thought isn't enough to make me panic, for the first time in my life . . . I have fashion block. Like writer's block. I go into my closet and I'm overwhelmed."

"I feel like that every day," Taylor said to Grace. "But I've never seen Lynn like this. This is a true fashion emergency."

"We can try to help," Grace said. "I have an idea. Lynn, can we go in your closet?"

"Um . . ." That was a big question. Nobody but Taylor had ever been in my closet. I looked at Grace, so ready to help me.

"We won't touch anything," Taylor reassured me. "You stay there till your nails and mask dry."

I watched as they opened my closet. And then I heard loud gasps.

"This is amazing!" Grace said.

"I know! Check this out!" Taylor said. "Look at this purse! I love this! And this scarf! And—"

I forced myself to sit still while I heard them in my closet. I heard oohs and aahs and squeals.

"Um, guys?" I called out. "I think I'm dry. In fact, I think my face is about to crack off."

"Oh, Lynn!" Taylor stuck her head out of the closet. "I almost forgot about you. This place is hypnotizing."

Grace came out and said, "You know, maybe my idea wasn't so great after all. I was going to suggest we all put together outfits for you and you could get ideas. But I'm afraid to touch anything and mess it up."

"Please. Just go for it," I told them. "Anything is worth a try. I'll wash my face; you guys play."

I washed off my face mask and came out of the bathroom to see Taylor standing in front of me with a long pink cardigan I'd shredded the bottom of and added white pearly beads to.

"That would look good on you," I agreed. "And I have the perfect skirt to wear with it over there hanging on my door. I just finished dyeing it that color. It's dry."

"I just liked the sweater. I meant for *you*, not that I wanted to wear it." Taylor said. But she put the outfit on.

"Ooh, this does look good on me," Taylor said. "Much better than these leggings I wore to school today. Can someone tell me why nobody stopped me from wearing shiny leggings?"

"Leggings are hard to pull off, Tay, much less shiny ones," I said. "Don't take it personally. Besides, how old are those magazines you're reading? You may want to toss them."

"Why can't something that looks good on me come into fashion? Like muumuus," Taylor said. "Not that they look good, but they'd cover me up. Or capes. Can you bring capes back into fashion, Lynn?"

"Capes are pretty cool," I said thoughtfully. Hmm. Not the superhero kind, but the romantic black ones that people wore to balls while their horses and buggies pulled them through the snow. A chic mix of "vampire meets historical."

"Earth to Lynn?" Taylor said. "You're spacing!"

"Sorry," I said, snapping myself back to reality. "I'll see what I can do."

Then I noticed Grace holding up a piece of dark blue velvet.

"Grace!" I said. "You're right! That's you! Do you have recitals? That would make an awesome long skirt."

"You think? It's really glamorous," Grace said. She held the material up to herself. "I do have a piano recital coming up." I wrapped the material around her to show what a skirt would look like. I pulled a white ruffly shirt— I'd made the ruffles myself and put lace to make the cuffs flare out in a Victorian style—off my shelf and held it up to her.

Grace and Taylor started posing in my full-length mirror on my closet door.

"Wait! Stop!" Taylor suddenly said. "We're supposed to be here for *Lynn*. Now we're all dressed up, but Lynn's not! I knew it. Lynn's destiny is to dress people. Nobody can help *her*. At least *we're* not helping."

"Sorry, Lynn," Grace said.

"That's not true, you guys totally helped me," I said. "At least you got me *into* the closet. I couldn't bring myself to even go in here before. At least you calmed me down."

"Why not pick one of the outfits on the wall?" Grace said, examining my Wall of LynnSpiration. "Do you usually look at this for ideas?"

"Well, not first," I said.

"Then what do you do?" Taylor asked.

Well. What *do* I do?

First I put on some music. Then I go in my closet and look at all the colors and materials. *Then* I stare at my Wall of LynnSpiration. And then I sit down on one of the furry fuchsia carpet squares I'd laid down in my closet. Then I think about what kind of mood I'm in. I think about who I really, really am that day. I think about who I want to be that day. What's going to happen that day. What makes me happy. And then I make it fun and I—suddenly something in my closet caught my eye.

"Lynn? Helloo? Earth to Lynn?" Taylor's voice pierced my thoughts.

I blinked.

"I got it," I said slowly. Then I stood up. "I got it. You guys just helped me get it."

I went over and threw my arms around Taylor and Grace so we were in a group hug.

Then I had to take action before I lost the mood. I released my friends and ran over to one of the containers that held fabric. I started shuffling through the drawers, searching for something.

"I think that our work is done," I heard Taylor say. They left the closet quietly.

"What just happened?" I heard Grace ask.

I didn't hear the answer. I was too busy.

I tilted my head a little and smiled at my reflection in the locker mirror. This was pretty close to the smile in the picture my mom and I had chosen to send to *GIIT-ter Girl* last night. I smiled a little wider, thinking what my face would look like online. Online for the total public when the website launched. Tomorrow!

"Hi," someone said. Jacob had come up to his locker and was watching me smile at myself in the mirror.

"Oh! Um," I said. "I just had um, something . . . in my nose." *Wait! Gross!*

"I mean my teeth! That's why I'm smiling at myself."

Agh. As the final bell went off, I grabbed the books I needed and closed my locker door.

"Which way are you walking?" Jacob asked, shutting his locker door at the same time.

"I'm meeting my friend Taylor at her locker," I said. "Then we're going to FonDo."

"I'm going over there, too." Jacob walked alongside me. We walked a little farther in silence.

"So, uh, well. You're going to FonDo?" I asked. *Duh. He just told me that.*

"Yeah, but just to stop by really quick," he said. "I'm going to visit my grandmother after that."

"How nice." *Hello, brain? Are you in there? Say something normal, please?*

"You kind of remind me of her," he said.

I remind him of his grandmother? Not exactly what I was hoping for.

"My grandmother knits and makes cool stuff like you," he explained.

Oh, because she makes things. *Whew.*

"She used to make some pretty amazing clothes. But now she has arthritis in her hands, so she can't sew or knit anymore."

"That's really sad. I can't imagine not being able to make things," I said. "I mean, if I'm stressed out or bumming it makes me feel better. Or if I'm happy I make something for my friends. What I make shows how I'm feeling."

Did that sound stupid? That sounded stupid. Maybe Jacob will just ignore—

"I'm kinda like that with my music," Jacob said. "Whatever's in my head I kinda can get out through my music."

"You play music?" I said. "Cool."

"Well, I don't play it," he said. "I mix it. I make play-lists, do a little DJ thing. It's not like having a talent, like yours. Well anyway, I'm going this way, so maybe I'll see you later if you're going to FonDo."

I sneaked a look at him as he walked down the hall. He was cute and he had called me talented. Now, that didn't happen every day. I needed that little burst of confidence, and I needed to hold on to it for another twenty-four hours or so, until the *GlITter Girl Online* launch.

The online launch. It was all happening so fast. Today was pretty much my last day of being anonymous. The story, with my name and picture, would be going up on the site tomorrow. For tomorrow, when people would likely look at me, I had an amazing outfit planned to represent *GlITter Girl*. Today my outfit was kind of meh because I just threw it on. I was wearing a lace slip dress and tall black boots I'd scored off eBay. Nice pieces, but nothing I'd made, nothing very original.

"Hi." I walked up to Taylor and Grace, who were standing together at Taylor's locker.

The girl a couple of lockers down looked up, and I recognized her as the emo-looking girl who'd sat at the table behind us at FonDo.

"I love that shirt!" I said to her.

"I found it on that website you told me about." She shrugged. "It came up for sale in the secondhand section, and somehow I got to it before anyone else."

"It's so cool," I said. "You know what, it would look

really good with your jean jacket, but not the short black one, the medium denim one. Oh, and you could wear your silver-and-red belt. . . ."

The girl looked at me a little strangely.

"She notices clothes," Grace hurriedly told her. "Not just yours."

"Uh, okay," the girl said, and walked away.

"Yeah, I got a little carried away there, didn't I," I said quietly, turning back to Taylor and Grace. "Ahem. So! What else is new?"

"We have a lot to celebrate," announced Taylor, shutting her locker. "So let's go to FonDo. First off, Grace, tell Lynn about the concert."

"Oh, it's not a big deal," Grace said as we walked. "I got a flute solo."

"No big deal?" Taylor said. "Freshmen never get solos. That's huge!"

"No, what's huge is the *GlITter Girl* launch tomorrow," Grace said.

"This is your last day before everyone knows it's you," Taylor continued. "Here's to Lynn for no longer being invisible!"

"Well, I've never really been invisible," I protested, pointing to my clothes.

But she was right in a way. I had felt invisible in the sense that most people had never understood the real me. Or really cared to. I hoped that would change. But I was nervous that it would only make things worse.

"But you're right, I'm going to enjoy my last day of nobody knowing I made the shoe," I said. "And being anonymous."

We got to the door of FonDo, and as I opened the door I heard my name.

"Lynn Vincent? That's who made the shoe ??!!"

?! I shut the door quickly. And fled—around the building to the nearest hiding space, behind the Dumpster.

"Are you okay? What happened?" Taylor said, rounding the corner after me. Grace followed her.

"I swear I just heard Chasey Welch say my name and that I made the shoe," I said.

"Do you think the IT panel found out already?" Taylor asked.

"Please say no," I said. "I'm just not prepared yet."

"Sorry, Lynn," Grace said, holding up her iPhone. "It's not just the IT panel. It looks like everyone's finding out. The website is launched."

She handed me her phone.

* * *

GlITterGirl.com
WELCOME TO OUR NEW WEBSITE!

Go behind the Seams with *GlITter Girl* as we travel the USA and discover our first IT Girl!

A LYNN-derella Story

It all started with a SHOE. We discovered the SHOE and fell in love. But we didn't know who made it, so we set out on a search for its creator. And that's when we found our first IT Girl.

Living in a small town, Lynn Vincent has expressed her fashion creativity, but not always to rave reviews.

"Sometimes people don't always get me," Lynn told us. "Actually, people here pretty much never get me. But I'm just trying to express myself through my clothes."

Well, we at *GlITter Girl* get her . . . and we think she's Lynn-credible!

She not only made the incredible shoe on our website, she's made clothes for her adorable pug, her BFF and of course herself. She has a closet where she designs her creations, complete with a "Wall of LynnSpiration"! Well, we're Lynn-spired!

Check out the photos of Lynn in her covetable "creations"!

Congratulations to Lynn Vincent, GlitterGirl.com's first GlITter Girl!

LYNN IS IN!

Want to be our next GlITter Girl IT Girl? E-mail us!

· · · · · · · · · · · · · ·

I stared at the picture of myself standing in my closet. My smile looked a little weird.

But my new cape was especially fabulous. Taylor had said she wanted to bring capes back. So I wanted to try to do my best and wear one in my IT Girl picture for her. The IT Girl picture that was now online for everyone to see. I was going to surprise Taylor with it, as well as a new capelet I'd made for her. But now, I was the one surprised.

"I need to regroup," I said, starting to hyperventilate. "I've got to go home, get out of here before anyone sees me."

"Lynn, you shouldn't hide," Grace said. "This is very exciting! They called it a LYNN-derella story! I love that."

"It's just that I'm not prepared for this," I said. "I was gearing up for full panic tomorrow, not today."

"Look, I can call my mom and see if she can pick us up," Taylor said. "Or maybe we can check if Dex can give you a ride home."

"I'll go in and talk to your brother," Grace said. "Since people will see Taylor and think of Lynn."

Grace left, and Taylor took out her phone. "I can't get

a signal over here to call my mom. Must be the Dumpster blocking my cell," she said.

As Taylor walked toward the front of the building, I leaned against the wall and took a deep breath. Oh, ew, it smelled terrible. Okay, maybe this was a little stupid. A lot stupid. I was hiding out by a Dumpster. But I'd meant it when I said I wasn't prepared. What I really wasn't ready for was people looking at me. And wondering "Why her?" I wished someone would come and tell me I could handle it.

"Lynn?"

I turned around. And there was Jacob.

"Are you okay?" he asked. "What are you doing behind the Dumpster?"

"Uh, recycling?" I answered. I stepped away from the Dumpster.

Okay, this was too weird. How likely was it that just at the moment I was hiding out from everyone at FonDo behind a Dumpster hoping for someone to make me feel better, Jacob Elias would happen to stumble across me. Was it fate?

"I ran into your friend Taylor over on the corner and she told me you were back here," Jacob said.

Oh. That was a little more realistic.

"Ew," Jacob said. "It stinks back here. Seriously, why are you back here?"

"Well, you're going to find out in a minute anyway. I'm hiding because I made the shoe," I said.

There. I'd told someone. I waited for the reaction.

"Uh, translation?" Jacob said. "You did what?"

"Remember how they were looking for the person who made that shoe? The one you said looked like something I'd wear? Not only would I wear it, but I made it," I said. "And once I told the magazine I'd made it, *GlITter Girl* wanted to put it on their website, and I'm the very first IT Girl for *GlITter Girl Online*. I thought it was going to be tomorrow, but the website just launched, so I'm hiding here."

Jacob blinked.

"Whoa," he said. "I was not expecting that. Whoa."

"I'm sure a lot of people aren't," I sighed.

"You really made that shoe?" Jacob said. When I nodded, he went on, "That is the coolest thing. I'm impressed."

Well. *Well, thank you,* I thought.

"You should be proud of yourself," Jacob said. "Not hiding behind a Dumpster."

"I'm sort of freaked out by the whole thing," I admitted. "I choked."

"Come on, I'll walk in with you to FonDo. You should be pumped," Jacob said.

I looked at him. Into his dark eyes that had little flecks of gorgeous blue in them. He would look really good in a darker shade of blue than the shirt he had on, which would bring out the flecks in them.

"I was thinking of just going home," I said. "Stalling. Gearing up for all those people looking at me."

"You have to do it sometime," he said. "Besides, no of-fense, but aren't you used to people looking at you?"

"Well, yeah," I said. "Obviously I stand out, and people look at me. But now they'll look and wonder what the heck *GlITter Girl* was thinking. I mean, they're calling me their IT Girl."

"Everyone in FonDo is sitting there thinking they're stupid for not knowing that," Jacob said. "Now everyone will appreciate you."

"I don't know about that," I said. "But thanks for the pep talk."

"It's kind of obvious that the IT Girl shouldn't be hid-ing behind a Dumpster. Come on."

"Wait," I said. "Do I smell like Dumpster? That would be bad if I made my debut smelling like Dumpster. Be honest."

"You're good." He grinned. "Just come on. I'll protect you."

Um. Okay, then. We walked around to the front, where Taylor was on the phone.

"I can't get hold of my mom," Taylor said, frustrated. "I left her a message and a text."

"It's okay," I said. "I'm going to try to go into FonDo."

Besides, maybe I'd been overreacting. Maybe people had found out and it had already blown over like it was no big deal. I took a deep breath and walked through the door of FonDo.

It's her!"

It *was* a big deal. People swiveled around in their seats and looked at me. Perhaps this was a mistake, to come in here after all. I shot Taylor a panicked look.

"There's Grace in the back talking to your brother," Taylor said. Then she lowered her voice. "Smile, just keep a smile on your face and let's go."

"Okay," I said. I plastered a smile on my face.

"Everyone's going to be psyched for you," Jacob turned around to say. "They'll all think it's cool."

"Jacob! Over here, man!" A French fry came flying our way. Some guy yelled from one of the popular-area tables near the front.

"Go ahead," I told him.

"You guys come with me," he said.

I looked at the table crowded with cheerleaders and jock

prep types. Obviously not my usual welcome committee.

"No, that's okay," I said. "We left our friend Grace kinda hanging. I see her in the back."

Taylor started quickly walking to the back. I followed her but was quickly blocked by Chasey Welch.

"You?" Chasey demanded. "*You* made the shoe?"

"Lynn did make the shoe," Taylor said defensively. "So ha! All those times you were making fun of her, Lynn was—"

"Hey, Tay," I interrupted before she could get in Chasey's face. I didn't think any good could come of that. "Can you go back with Grace? I'll be right there."

I turned back to Chasey and maneuvered so Taylor was blocked.

"I thought it was a joke at first," Chasey said, shaking her head. She looked at me with squinty eyes. "You made the shoe and now you're on the website as the IT Girl?"

"Chasey, I can't believe you!" Chasey's friend Kayden had popped up behind her. "You guys are so cool! You did such a good acting job!"

"What?" Chasey and I both said, confused.

"Remember when you got the text saying who the IT Girl was, and she was sitting right there with us? And you guys both pretended you didn't know anything?"

"Oh. Oh yeah." Chasey looked at me uncomfortably.

"So you knew it was this Lynn girl the whole time!" Kayden said. "And you were sworn to secrecy, so to hide the secret you made fun of her instead? Wow, you guys are good actresses."

Heh.

"I know," Chasey said, trying to roll with it. "I mean, we had to totally cover it up. Yeah. So I need to, uh, make a call. Come on, Kayden."

"Wait, I want details," Kayden said. "How come they picked her and not you, Chasey? Are you next, Chasey?"

I had to smile at that one, which gave me the courage to walk to the back of FonDo and ignore the people looking at me. Taylor and Grace were sitting at our usual table near the girls' room, talking urgently to Dex.

"I was just going to send Dex to rescue you," Taylor said. "I feel so bad Chasey ambushed you like that."

"My shift's up in fifteen minutes," Dex said. "I can give you a ride home if you can hang out."

"Do you want to go back to the Dumpster?" Grace asked. "We'll hide with you."

"No, the worst is over," I said. "I survived, and now I just want a mochaccino." Taylor and Grace ordered drinks, too, and I turned my chair so it was facing the bathroom wall and away from the rest of the place.

"See? It's all no big deal. We can stay back here in peace and quiet," I said. "Just the three of us like normal."

"Um, Lynn?" Grace gestured me to turn around.

Chasey was standing behind me, with her hands on her hips.

"What are you doing in the back of FonDo, Lynn?" Chasey asked me. "We're saving your seat."

Gee, why is that? Hmm . . . Perhaps since you discovered

to your shock and dismay that I'M the Very First IT Girl. Well, missy, I'm not going to desert my friends for shallow, superficial people like you.

"No thanks." I leaned back in my chair confidently. "I'm staying back here with my friends."

"Oh, your friends won't mind," Chasey said even more confidently. "You should be sitting with us."

"Chasey, I'm not leaving my friends," I said. "And you know what, I'm not leaving my table. I've come to love our table in the back. It's perfect."

There was a loud flush from the girls' room. I ignored it. I was standing my ground.

"Hmm," Chasey said. She squinted at me again. Then she flipped her hair and walked back up to the front.

"Ha!" I said to Taylor and Grace. "I just struck a blow for Not-IT Girls everywhere. In my own teeny tiny way."

"Oh, go ahead," Taylor said. "It's inevitable."

"Taylor, what are you talking about?" I said.

"Well, you're the IT Girl now," Taylor said, looking miserable. "You're not a loser or a freak anymore. We're going to lose you to the Popular People."

"Taylor!" I said. "You don't seriously believe that."

"Yes. Chasey's going to be your new BFF. You'll go shopping together and all dress fabulously and sit at their table at FonDo," she said.

"Stop it," I said. "Taylor, you have serious Popular People issues. Well, I know Grace doesn't think that. Right, Grace?"

"Well," Grace said. "Some people do want to be popular. I don't get it, if it means being stuck with people like that Chasey. But don't let us hold you back if that's what you want to do."

"GUYS!" I said, raising my voice. "Hello? I'm not deserting you for the Popular People. I'm loyal to my friends! I'm proud to be a person in the back!"

I pounded my hand on the table for emphasis. There. If I was going to be an IT Girl, I was going to do it on my own terms.

And then I heard clapping behind me. I turned around. The girls at the emo table behind me were clapping.

"Nice speech," the girl who'd worn the VintageBette shirt said to me.

"Thanks," I said. "And I mean it."

"Hey, I know you," Taylor said to the girl. "Did you ever take ballet in elementary school? Are you Charlotte?"

"Yeah, I was. Now I'm Char, short for Chartreuse. But I've blacked both ballet and that name out of my memory," Char said.

"Ugh, ballet wasn't for me either," Taylor agreed. "I'm still scarred from when that girl in our class told me I looked like a plump pink pig in my leotard."

"Oh yeah," Charlotte said, shaking her head. "She kept oinking. Ugh. Anyway, Lynn, thanks for sticking up for all of us in the back."

"Yeah!" a guy from her table said. "We're sick of those girls acting like the people in the back of FonDo are total losers."

"No, seriously," Char said. "We're not total rejects just because we can't sit at the good tables at lunch."

"Or because we want to sit in the front seats in the classroom!" a guy wearing an Einstein T-shirt said.

Everyone was like, Yeah!!!

"See?" I said to Taylor and Grace. This was pretty cool. Power to the people. People were bonding all over. "We can have fun without the Popular People. Without worrying about Chasey and her putdowns and her rudeness and her superiority complex and thinking she can push everyone around—"

"You're right," Taylor said. "Except one thing. Chasey's coming back."

I turned around to see that Chasey was indeed coming back, this time flanked by Kayden and Kyla. Chasey was smiling and talking on her cell as she walked to our table. She stole a chair from the emo girl table and sat down with us. Kayden and Kyla stood right nearby.

"Okay, people!" The manager of FonDo was walking over to the geek table. "We've had to do a little rearranging here. Sorry to inconvenience you, but some of you will have to move to different tables."

Some of the FonDo servers started moving the food from the emo table, the geek table, some other tables around me.

Then I saw Chasey put her purse down in front of Char.

"Hey! I'm sitting here!" Char said.

"The manager will explain why you have to move," Chasey said.

The manager went over to talk to Char. Before I knew what was going on, everyone was moved from the tables in the back. The servers were wiping the tables down. Except our table.

"What's going on?" Grace asked.

"I dunno. I guess we all have to move," I said, getting up.

"Silly, sit right back down, Lynn," Chasey said.

And then, all of a sudden, a huge group of people descended, taking over the newly empty tables next to us. Populars, jocks, and a confused-looking Arin Morgan.

"Arin, sit by me!" Chasey said, patting a seat next to her. "The IT panel should stick together. Where's our server?" she grumbled. "What's up with this service?"

"I'll go find one," Arin said, getting up. I didn't blame her for wanting to escape this chaos. With all these Popular People squashing me, I started to feel slightly claustrophobic.

"Lynn, do you have any gum?" Chasey asked.

"Uh, Chasey? What's going on?" I asked her.

"You didn't want to sit up front." Chasey shrugged. "So we're all moving back here with you."

"I can hear a toilet flushing," Kyla whined.

Chasey gave her a look. "Look how nice and private it is back here. It's like the VIP room at a club—they're always in the back. Just like we are."

I couldn't help notice Taylor's eyes light up.

"Totally!" Kayden was saying. "We should make Fon-Do have a sign saying 'VIP Section'!"

Okay, this was getting ridiculous.

"Good idea!" Chasey said. "Go tell the server."

"It *is* more private back here," said some girl sitting on her boyfriend's lap. They started kissing. Oh no! It was the Makeout Couple from my locker!

"So, everyone knows my friend Lynn," Chasey announced loudly. "Lynn, you probably recognize everybody."

Everyone except the Makeout Couple looked at me.

"Um, hi," I said. "These are my friends Taylor and—"

"So, Lynn," Chasey interrupted. "Tell everyone how fab it is that we're doing this *GlITter Girl* stuff together."

"Um yeah, fab," I said.

"That was a good story about you," a girl said. "I was excited to find out the Mystery Shoe Girl goes to our very own school."

"Well, the article was a little dramatic," Chasey said. "Saying that nobody really understood her. When she has fellow fashionistas like me who have supported her since forever."

Oh, gag. I couldn't take the charade anymore.

"Supported me?" I said, turning to her. "You—"

"Lynn!" someone cut me off. "How did you think of making that shoe?"

"When is your shoe going to be in stores?"

"Did they mention Independence High in the article?"

Then someone asked, "Does this all seem really weird?"

Finally a question I knew the answer to. I looked around. I was surrounded by all these people. Taylor looked thrilled.

Grace was looking more than slightly overwhelmed, probably due to the basketball player who apparently couldn't find a chair, so was sitting on her lap. I noticed my brother in conversation with Arin Morgan near the front.

"Yeah," I said out loud. "Really, really weird."

S he not only made the incredible shoe on our website, she's made clothes for her adorable pug,'" I read off the website out loud. "Look, Bella, they call you adorable. You're famous."

Bella cocked her head as she looked at me from the bed. She was wearing a red-and-black plaid flannel pajama shirt I'd made for her.

I went back to the site and grinned at my picture. After the chaos of FonDo, it was nice to come home and collect my thoughts.

"'Well, *we* at *GlITter Girl* get her . . . and think she's LYNN-genius,'" I read to Bella. That was my favorite line of all. No wait, maybe my favorite line was this:

"'You voted and you love it! You've given THE SHOE 5 stars out of 5 stars! To see the shoe close-up, click the link!'"

I clicked on the link and my shoe popped up. I clicked on all the pop-up pictures and sighed, content. It just never got old. Suddenly, a really weird smell wafted into my bedroom. I looked up and saw Dex standing at the door holding a bowl of . . . of . . . something.

"What are you eating?" I asked him. "It smells disgusting."

"It's ramen noodles mixed with peanut butter," Dex said. "And some chocolate chips."

"Ew," I said. "Just ew."

"Mom's gonna be a little late," Dex said. "She said you could wait or you can nuke something for dinner if you want. I made extra of this if you want some."

"I just lost my appetite," I said. "I'll wait. I ate at Fon-Do anyway. Thank your manager for the fruit plate, by the way."

"Yeah, how about that," he said. "My manager never gives away anything for free. She was, like, 'Everyone who's with Lynn gets free fruit!' The fruit has to be thrown out anyway if nobody orders it, but still. She was bummed, though, that you left before she got your autograph. I told her I'd get it for you."

"And you got to talk to Arin Morgan, I noticed," I teased him. "I saw you guys talking!"

"She's nice," Dex mumbled. "She also said she liked my shirt. That one you made for me. So you know, thanks."

I watched Dex leave the room. I was glad to see he had some social success today, too. It was weird how much had changed in school after just one day. I was sure the novelty of me being cool would wear off soon, so I'd enjoy it while it lasted.

Speaking of friends, I decided to leave a message for Taylor on her Facebook. I noticed I had messages in my in-box and friends who wanted to be added. I opened the Add Friends and whoa! I had thirty-seven new friend requests? Usually I had zero. Or one or two, but then they were both creepy spam people. So I hesitated before I clicked on the first one. Could people have tracked me down from *GlITter Girl*? No, I didn't use my last name. I skimmed the list. It was a bunch of people from school. I recognized a girl from my gym class. I'd never talked to her before, but hey, I was open to new friends. I accepted. Hey, there was a girl who hadn't spoken to me since second grade. ACCEPT. Hey, that girl's a senior! ACCEPT. I couldn't help myself. I was feeling a little Pop.U.Lar with all these new "friends."

And well, looky here. Chasey Welch. Chasey wanted to be my friend. Hehehehe. And Tehehehe. Should I click DENY? No, I probably shouldn't, because of the IT panel. But I definitely wasn't going to click ACCEPT right away. Let her sweat it out.

Oh, then there was Kayden and Kyla. I clicked ACCEPT. Just to freak out Chasey a little. Hehehe. This was pretty fun.

And then Taylor called my cell.

"Omigosh, how much did FonDo totally rock today?" Taylor was practically shrieking. "It was the coolest!! You're a rock star!!"

"Okay, you're weirding me out," I said.

"Sorry," Taylor said. "I'll be calm. But come on, how

cool was it to have all those people trying to sit with us? The most people I ever had even at the New Student Table was six, and that was the first day of school."

"It was crazy," I agreed. "I'm glad you enjoyed it. Things are still weird. Like, I got thirty-seven new friend requests on Facebook. Real people from school, not spam."

"No way!" Taylor said. "Hey, I wonder if they'll add me, too. I'll have to go on and try. Also, do you need a ride to school tomorrow morning? My mom's all, like, 'Did I see you and Lynn talking to Chasey Welch?' And then I told her how everyone wanted to sit with you, so she told me to ask you."

"Well, that's one benefit, I guess," I said. "Your mom will let you be seen with me in public now."

"Oh please, *she* wants to be seen with you in public," Taylor said. "She was bragging to her friends. I think I'm about to be traded in as a daughter."

I thought about being Mrs. Snyder's daughter and shuddered. Uh, no thanks.

"Well, I'll take the ride to school," I said. "Any chance to avoid the bus."

"Besides, you need a chauffeur now that you're famous," Taylor said. "And you need a bodyguard; I can do that. No wait, I can be your personal assistant! All the stars have personal assistants! What do personal assistants do? Can I be yours?"

"Taylor!" I was laughing. "Stop it. You can be my *best friend*."

"Okay," she said. "But don't go hiring a personal assistant without asking me first. Well, I better go. I have to go figure out what to wear tomorrow."

"Do you need help?" I said.

"No, I don't want to bother you or anything. But then again, if I'm going to be seen with you tomorrow, you probably want me to look good," Taylor said. "Ugh, I make a terrible BFF of the newest IT Girl. You're probably going to dump me soon for Chasey."

"I wouldn't be too concerned," I said. "No matter what, you're my best friend. Besides, you know all my secrets and could leak them to the tabloids."

"Oh yeah," she giggled. "Remember when you created that black lace water-balloon bra?"

"Yeek! I'm hanging up on you now," I said.

"Wait! I take it back! Please tell me what to wear tomorrow!" Taylor said.

I closed my eyes and leaned back in my chair.

"Okay, just wear a white tank and your first-day-of-school jeans," I said. "Your pink Chucks."

"Uh, that's it? Won't I be a little blah? And cold?" Taylor asked.

"Come five minutes early and I'll do the rest," I said. "Trust me."

I already had my outfit for tomorrow picked out. So that gave me a little extra time in my closet to work on something else.

L ynn, I'm more than happy to pick you up for school tomorrow, too," Mrs. Snyder called to me in the back-seat of her car. "I know your mother has it so hard being a single parent, poor thing, so I'm happy to help."

"Oh, that's okay," I said. "I don't want you to go out of your way."

"No, I insist," she said. "And it will give you and Taylor some bonding time."

"Say yes," Taylor hissed at me under her breath. "*Say yes.*"

Taylor had told me on the way to school that when I wasn't around, her mother gave her "Life Lessons." Which basically were: lose weight, act cooler, and make new friends who weren't Lynn. Although the last one would now be dropped off the lecture due to my alleged IT status.

"Thank you, Mrs. Snyder," I said. "That'd be great."

Taylor breathed a sigh of relief.

"I love the sweater you brought for Tay-tay; it's simply precious," Mrs. Snyder said.

I'd brought Taylor the cardigan she'd tried on in my closet. And I'd replaced the buttons with some big pink ones and then I'd painted a little teeny BFF on each button. I'd accessorized her with some pink homemade friendship bracelets.

And me? I was wearing a full satin pink skirt, with lime green exposed zippers on it along the waist and along the hem. I had tucked the hem so that the green tulle, a slightly paler green, was exposed underneath. It was a masterpiece. I wore a top that was two shades of pink lighter and lime green embroidery on it that said LyVin. And pink friendship bracelets like Taylor's.

"Hellooo? Earth to IT Girl! We're at school!" Taylor said.

I snapped out of it. The car was pulling up at the school drop-off point.

"Thanks, Mrs. Snyder," I said, and got out of the car. Taylor got out behind me.

"I'll pick you up tomorrow, Lynn!" she was saying as she drove away. "Taylor, dear! Pat your hair down on the left side!"

"Can we slow down a little?" Taylor said as we started walking into school. She slowed her pace.

"Sure." I shrugged. We walked along slowly. Realllly

slowly. Taylor stopped to fix her shoelaces. Then she stopped to adjust her socks.

"Are you okay?" I asked her.

Just then some girls came walking up really quickly.

"Lynn? Taylor?" one of them asked. "Hiiii! It's so nice to meet you guys!"

"Um, hi?" I said. The girls started walking with us. I looked at Taylor, who gave me a guilty face.

"Lynn, it's me, Emily Liz, from Facebook."

"And I'm Marifer, you added me last night, remember?!" the other girl said. "Is that the outfit you put together for Taylor? I love that sweater!"

Oh! These were some of the friends I'd added on Facebook. I recognized Emily Liz from her photo. But how did they know about the outfit? I looked at Taylor for explanation.

"Um, we were chatting last night," Taylor said. She lowered her voice. "Sorry, I got carried away adding your friends. I, uh, mentioned I was your best friend and you were picking my outfit, but I didn't tell them anything else, I swear. I was just so happy to have more than just you as my friend. Grace isn't allowed to have a Facebook."

"Sorry we were late to meet you guys," Marifer was saying. "I couldn't decide which shoes to wear. What do you think, Lynn? Do these shoes work with this outfit?"

I shot Taylor a look.

"They wanted to meet you, so . . ." Taylor whispered.

"You could have warned me," I said out of the side of

my mouth to her. Then I raised my voice to talk to Marifer. "I think your shoes are cute, don't you?"

"But do *you* like them?" she asked. "I mean, I totally value your opinion. You're the IT Girl."

"I can't believe a real live *GlITter Girl* IT Girl goes to my school," Emily Liz sighed.

We walked up to the door.

"I'll get the door for you." Emily Liz held open the door.

"Thanks," I said. And then it got crazy.

"Look! It's her!" Some other girls spotted me and came over. "We saw you on the website! You look sooo cute!"

"I love the shoe," someone said. "It seriously is the coolest shoe I've ever seen."

"Thanks!" I said. I did love to hear that.

People were waving and saying hi to me as I walked by. Well, alrighty, this was definitely different. A group of people walked with me and Taylor all the way to my locker.

"Uh, that's my locker," I said loudly, pointing. "You all probably have to go to homeroom now, right?"

"I'm going down this hall! I'll see you at lunch, Lynn," Taylor said. "Bye!"

"Bye, Tay!" I called after her as she walked down the hall. Everyone followed me over to my locker.

As usual, the Makeout Couple was going at it.

"Move it! You're blocking Lynn Vincent's locker," Emily Liz commanded. The Makeout Couple looked up, startled. And moved down a few lockers before they started kissing again.

Hmm, maybe having fans would have its good points. The girls all crowded around my locker as I was opening it.

"Love your locker decorations!" exclaimed a girl who didn't look even remotely familiar.

"I wish my locker was so cool!" another girl said.

Everyone squealed again.

"Excuse me, excuse me," I heard someone say. "May I get to my locker, please?"

Jacob! I could hear him, but I couldn't see him through the group of girls standing around me. Nobody was moving.

"Guys!" I said. "Someone needs to get to his locker here."

"Back off, girls!" Emily Liz shouted. "Let the *GlITter Girl*'s friend get to his locker." They all took a step back so there was a little open space around me and Jacob.

"You are so lucky you have the locker right next to Lynn Vincent," someone said to him.

Jacob looked at me, an eyebrow raised.

I tried to say something, but the crowd surrounded me. I saw Jacob shut his locker and head to class.

The warning bell rang.

"Lynn! Which way are you going? I'll walk you to class!" I was swept away.

Lynn, I love your skirt," the girl walking next to me said. "Did you make that yourself?"

"Yeah, and thanks." I said. For the thousandth time today. Every time I walked down the hall someone said something nice about my clothes. Not that I was complaining. I appreciated the compliments. But it was a little distracting to be stopped so much.

"Lemme check out your shoes! Did you make those, too?"

"Cute sweatery-shirt-ripped-up thing."

I noticed that one came from a girl who had previously called me a freak. I said another thank-you just as the warning bell for the period rang, and the girls who'd been following me scurried to class.

"Lynn, you're going to be late!" one of them cautioned me.

"She's the IT Girl," someone answered. "She's above the rules."

Well, that certainly wasn't true. But I was willing to be late to first-period lunch just to get a few moments alone. I didn't think the principal would really get me into trouble today, since, as she'd put it when she called me down to her office to congratulate me, I was "a shining example of putting the Independence in Independence High School."

Then she'd asked me which color suit she should wear to some principals' convention. I vetoed both her kelly green and her fuchsia choices, and she'd seemed grateful when I suggested dark gray with a burgundy scarf to bring out her skin tones. So I figured she owed me one.

Speaking of owing, I saw someone I owed an apology to. Char, from the emo table, was walking past me.

"Hey!" I stopped her. "I'm sorry about the whole having-to-move-tables situation at FonDo."

"It's fine," Char assured me. "Actually, we ended up sitting with the computer guys. They were cool. I've got a date with one of them tonight."

"Oh, wow," I said.

"Plus, it was cool to finally get a decent table up front," she said. "No flushing toilet noises, you know."

"I haven't even gotten to sit up front," I told her. "Well, I'm glad we're cool."

I still couldn't believe I was now known as the IT Girl. Me, Lynn Vincent. I'd walked the halls without one weird look. Without anyone calling me a freak or rolling their eyes at my outfit. Not that I was complaining but . . . All morning, I'd been surrounded by people. I'd been congratulated, complimented, and crowded. I hadn't had time to figure out how to handle this.

How had things changed so dramatically in one day? I mean, the same people who called me a freak yesterday were now gushing about the same clothes??!

"Hey!"

I jumped. Jacob was standing at his locker. He had on a deep blue rugby shirt that brought out the blue flecks in his dark eyes. He was just so very preppy today. Yet his retro sneakers saved him from overpreppiness.

"I'm shocked to see you without your groupies," Jacob said. "The locker area's been crazy."

"Oh," I said. "Hah. Uh-huh. Uh."

Brilliant and witty response.

"Why aren't you in class?" I asked.

"I claimed I had to go to the bathroom, but it's really a cover. I forgot my math homework," he said. "How about you?"

"I have no excuse," I admitted. "I'm going to lunch, but I just needed a breather."

"From all the excitement?" he said. "You must be psyched."

"Yeah," I said, but it came out like a question.

"Wow, that's convincing," he said.

"No, I *am* psyched," I said. "Or at least I was until school today. This morning has weirded me out."

"Why?"

I couldn't really articulate it.

Two girls walked by and pointed at me. But they didn't laugh or roll their eyes. I heard the words *IT* and *shoe* as they passed.

"See?" I said. "That kind of thing?"

"I think it's awesome," Jacob said. "You deserve the recognition. And like we talked about, you're used to attention."

"Oh come on," I said. "You read the article. You know what kind of attention I usually get. I'm used to people *insulting* me because of my outfits. But now suddenly since *GlITter Girl* recognized me, they're complimenting me. Isn't that . . . hypocritical?"

Jacob shut his locker and leaned against it.

"Yeah," he said thoughtfully. "I guess it is."

"See!" I said. "So how am I supposed to react? I'm just supposed to walk around all day and just smile and say thank you to people who were taunting me a week ago?"

"Sure, why not? You've earned it." Jacob shrugged. "You might as well enjoy it. Like that quote, living well is the best revenge. I guess you could get revenge by ignoring them or insulting them or whatever. But it doesn't seem like that's really you. Unless I'm totally wrong and you secretly want to be one of those girls who think they're all that and make fun of everyone else."

"No! I definitely don't."

"Then use your powers for good, not evil," he said.

"Remember, you're a LynnSpiration! You can go Lynn-Spire people!"

"Okay, you can stop that," I laughed. "I get the point."

"Good, then my work here is done," he said. "I better get back to math before Mr. Bumbrey does his usual 'What took you so long, did you fall in?' routine. And then we all have to laugh."

Jacob folded up his math homework and stuck it in his pocket.

"See you," I said. I watched him walk down the hall. He turned the corner and was out of sight.

Well. Well. Well. Well.

I grinned as I picked up my tote bag. Suddenly I felt more than ready for lunch.

A girl came down the hall. I saw the recognition in her eyes as she saw me. She ducked her head shyly as she walked past me.

"Hey," I called to her. "I like your shoes."

"Really? You do?" she said, and smiled. "Thanks, Lynn."

Hmm. LynnSpiring.

I smiled a little, too. La-la-la. Okay, yes. What was there not to smile about? Jacob was right. It was all good. Even though I'd endured years of torment, I could rise above it. And he called me awesome. Heh!

I hurried down the hall so I could at least be there for part of lunch. Even IT Girls needed to eat, right? Well, I guess some IT Girls didn't eat, but that wasn't the look or the health habit I was going for.

I entered the lunchroom and headed toward the table where Taylor and I sat alone. Scratch that, *used* to sit alone. Our lunch table was full. *No, overflowing.*

"There she is!" someone said. "She's here!"

"Lynn!" Taylor waved to me. "We were waiting for you!"

"I saved you a seat!" Some girl I never saw before in my life was calling me. "Sit here!" She elbowed some poor girl out of the seat next to her.

"That's okay," I said. "I'll just share with Taylor."

Taylor scooched over.

Do we know these people? I whispered to her. I guess that was good I didn't recognize them. That probably meant they hadn't insulted me, at least recently.

"Let me introduce you to everyone," Taylor said loudly. "That's Kate, Marieke, you met Emily Liz and Marifer this morning . . ."

"Hi," I said to everyone. "I'm Lynn."

"*We know!*" everyone squealed.

"What are you having for lunch today?" someone asked me.

"Uh, turkey in a tortilla wrap," I said. "An apple. And my mom's brownies."

"Ooh, I love turkey!" someone squealed.

"I have an apple, too!" someone else said.

Uh. Okay. That's not unusual, but . . . I took a bite out of my wrap. Everyone watched me chew. Nobody spoke. I felt like everyone could hear me chewing. I hoped I didn't look gross. This was awkward.

"Taylor," one of them said, "can we ask her now?"

"Lynn," Taylor said, "do you mind if they ask you some questions?"

LynnSpiring.

"Go for it," I said.

"One question per person," Taylor said. She looked at me. "We figured out a system before you came. Marifer is up first."

Marifer cleared her throat.

"Where can I buy the shoes?" Marifer asked.

"Well, actually you can't," I said. "There's just the one pair."

"Why aren't you wearing the shoes?" Marieke asked.

"The *GlITter Girl* office has the shoe," I said. "They're going to give it back to me when they're done using it."

"Will we get to see them?" Marieke asked.

"Ahem," Taylor said. "You've already asked your question. One per customer."

"Uh, that's okay—" I started to say, but Taylor shushed me.

"My turn. How many famous people have you met?" Emily Liz asked.

"Well, I met Valentyna, and she's a famous fashion person," I said. "But no celebrities."

"Yet, anyway," Taylor said. "She's just started."

I gave Taylor a look like *What are you talking about?* She just smiled back.

"Okay, my turn. Lynn, do you like my outfit?" Kate asked.

"Um," I said. I looked at her outfit. This was touchy. I

didn't want to offend anyone here. "Well. It doesn't matter what I think. As long as *you* like it."

"But I don't," Kate said glumly. "I pretty much never like what I'm wearing."

"Oh, I am so there with you," Taylor said. "If it weren't for Lynn and her fashion advice, I'd look like a walking freakazoid."

"Lynn gives you fashion advice?" Kate asked. "But you guys have such . . . different styles."

"You mean because I dress crazy and Taylor is normal?" I laughed.

"No! I didn't mean—!" Kate stammered.

"It's okay," I said. "That's what I mean. I know you don't want to dress like me. I know *nobody* wants to dress like me. Except me."

"Actually, *I've* always thought you looked really unique," Kate said. "Even though I know people thought it was weird. At least you're not boring like me. I just don't want to look . . . schlumpy anymore. I need help."

"She does," Marieke said. "And as her very best friend in the world, I mean that in the nicest way possible. Please, Lynn. Help her."

Kate looked at me. Everyone looked at me. She was wearing a sweatshirt and ill-fitting jeans. I looked around for inspiration. The cafeteria tables were busy. Except for one long empty table off to the corner that had several tablecloths in our school colors: red and white.

"Anyone know what that's for?" I asked.

"The pep team had something set up before," said Kate.

I got up, looked around, and snagged two tablecloths—a red and a white. As everyone watched, I took out my scissors and chopped a piece off the white tablecloth. I knotted and tied it and did some quick handstitching with my emergency sewing kit.

"What are you making?" Taylor finally asked.

"The paper lunch bags made me think of a paper bag skirt," I said. "So I'm making a paper bag–style skirt that's cute but not too radical. Plus, Kate, you have the perfect legs for it."

"Really?" She looked skeptical, but took it to the girls' room when I was done with it.

"My turn! My turn!" Emily Liz said. "Anything for me?"

Her pale yellow shirt wasn't doing her skin color any favors. I cut a long slice off the red tablecloth, fringed it, and made her a scarf.

"It brings out the color in your face," I said. "Little things can make a big difference."

Just then Kate came out, wearing the skirt. And a big happy smile on her face after she heard all the compliments about her cool new skirt. I finished her off by having her take off her sweatshirt and flipping it upside down to make a shrug.

"I look almost fashionable!" she squealed. "Lynn, you're amazing!"

Aw. Yay. The rest of lunch went by in a blur. I'd made something for all the girls at my table. I'd made a headband for Marieke out of the white tablecloth. I'd whipped up matching friendship bracelets for two BFFs out of the ties to our sandwich Baggies. The lunchroom theme was working for me. I considered snagging another tablecloth to make a cute wrap dress for myself at home, too.

"You look so good!" I heard one of the girls say to Emily Liz as she was dumping her lunch tray. "Definitely wear red tomorrow."

Wow. This was pretty fun. People complimenting me and actually wanting fashion advice from me, the weirdly dressed freshman freak. And people actually wearing clothes I made, even from tablecloths. I could get used to this.

"Come on, Lynn!" the girls called for me to join them on their way out. Yup, it was nice to have people want to actually be seen with me.

I picked up my lunch tray and my tote bag and started to stand up, but I didn't get very far. Somehow I was stuck. I craned my neck to look and realized one of my zippers was stuck in the fold of the metal chair. Crud. I sat back down and tried to subtly shift around so nobody would notice, but somehow I must have yanked the zipper off, and I heard a ripping noise.

Oh. No. I tried to check out the damage. I looked behind me and oh, there was definitely damage. I saw a long piece of satin and tulle on the ground and then, oh crud— a flash of bright green underwear. I sat back down again. The bell rang. Uh-oh, I was supposed to be in math class in five minutes.

"Come on, Lynn!" Taylor and the girls were waving.

I tried to smile and pretend like everything was just fine. I waved, Go on! Go on without me!

Nobody was going on. Crud, they all were coming over. And not just them. A whole crowd of people was coming my way. I squirmed in my seat to make sure I was covered.

Some girls came up and surrounded me. "I heard you're doing IT Girl makeovers! Can you make something for me?"

"I don't want to say no, but um, I have to get to class," I said.

"I'll walk with you," one of the girls said.

Uh. I wasn't moving from this seat. I needed help.

"Taylor?" I called through the crowd. "Where are you?"

"Excuse me, pardon me." I heard Taylor's voice coming through.

"Hey! I was here first," someone said.

"I'm Lynn's personal assistant! Lemme through!" Taylor said. She forced herself to the table.

"Fashion emergency," I said under my breath. "Involving underwear."

Taylor didn't miss a beat.

"People! People!" Taylor announced. "Lynn has a daily limit or, uh, her brain fries, but we'll have sign-ups at lunch tomorrow! Go to class!"

The warning bell rang.

Everyone started leaving to go to their classes, yelling that they'd see me for their makeovers.

"My brain fries?" I asked Taylor as I waited it out.

"I choked," Taylor said. "But I got rid of your fans, didn't I? I told you that you'd need a personal assistant. And apparently bodyguard."

"You better go or you'll be late to class," I said. "I have to wait till everyone leaves to figure this out."

"I'll wait with you," Taylor said as she watched the final stragglers leave. "I just have study hall next."

We waited until the room was empty and I showed her the damage.

"This needs major help," I sighed. "If you could block me till we get to the bathroom, I can try to fix it in there."

"Take my book bag," Taylor said. "It's huge. Hang it behind you and I'll stick close, too."

I held the bag behind me. It was insanely heavy from the fashion magazines she was still carrying around.

"I'm right behind you," Taylor said. "Now, walk."

I started walking quickly out the door. I could feel a breeze where my underwear was hanging out.

"Walk, walk, walk," Taylor directed. "Oh no! People coming up behind you! Go left! Turn!"

I turned awkwardly. I passed some people who gave me the *Look, it's the IT Girl* look. Hi, hi. Nothing unusual here. Nothing to see, carry on. Then I saw Chasey coming down the hall. I walked faster.

"Slow down!" Taylor said. "I can't keep up with you!"

"Chasey alert!" I said. I tried to turn down the hall, but it was too late.

"Lynn!" Chasey called out. "Wait up!"

Augh, what timing. I'd managed to avoid her all day. There was no escape. I leaned my back against a random locker. Taylor stood next to me, pretending we were just talking.

"Hi, Chasey," I said.

"Lynn, your skirt is too cute," Chasey said. "Guess what? The IT panel is getting together and I want to tell you all about it. Walk with me to class?"

"I need to stay here," I said. "And, uh . . ."

"Get something from my locker," Taylor finished brightly. She turned and started dialing a locker combination.

"Okay, then text me!" she said.

"Okay, I'll text you," I said, just to get rid of her. I watched her walk away and breathed a sigh of relief when she turned the corner. I turned back to Taylor, who was looking grumpy.

"What?" I asked her.

"You were pretty nice to her. 'Chasey, I'll text you!'" she mimicked me.

"Oh come on. It's not like I could turn around and ignore her, because I needed to keep my *back pressed up against this locker so my underwear isn't on display!*" I said.

"Ugh, you're right," Taylor said. "Ignore me. I'm especially sensitive today. My mother had coffee with Chasey's mother, and she's back on her 'Why isn't Taylor popular?' She even thinks you're great; now that you're the

IT Girl, it's like you're a celebrity. And I'm still a loser."

Taylor and I started walking, with her blocking my rear just in case.

"You're not a loser. And I'm not a celebrity," I said. "And that's a really good thing right now, because if I was, the paparazzi would have pictures of me flashing my underwear and everyone would think I did it on purpose. Ugh."

Taylor laughed.

"That *was* a major piece of fabric that ripped off," Taylor said. "Figures you had on your lime green happy frog underwear."

"Yeah," I said. "I felt like wearing a little humor underneath. And OH NO!"

A classroom door had opened and an entire class was heading our way!

"Turn! Turn!" Taylor urged. "There's a bathroom in hallway B! Walk faster! Faster!"

She started pushing me forward. I walked faster and faster, but I heard people behind us catching up.

"I need to take a breath!" I said, gasping. "Your backpack is heavy!"

"Lynn? Taylor?" Someone was coming out of a classroom. Whew! It was just Grace.

"Grace!" Taylor said. "We need help! Cover Lynn from behind!"

"Huh? Why?" Grace asked, and looked. And then said, "Ohhhh!"

"I know, humiliating," I said. "I need to get to a bathroom!"

"I have a better idea!" Grace said. "I have a closer place to hide."

She opened the door she'd come out of and shoved me into a room that had a pile of instruments and black cases.

"It's the music supply room," Grace said. "I only have the key because I was returning something from band. You should be safe here."

"Thanks, Grace," I said. "You saved me. You better get to class," I told Taylor and Grace. "You guys are way late."

We were not rule breakers. Pretty much the only rules I ever broke were fashion ones.

"Hey." Taylor shrugged. "If I get in trouble, I'll tell the principal that I was helping our school reputation."

"How is that?" I asked her.

"Duh, helping you avoid being one of those IT Girls who are in the papers for flashing their underwear."

"Good thing there's no paparazzi here," I laughed. I slid my skirt off and looked at it. "Wow, this is major damage. I have a sewing kit with me, but I wish I had some glue."

"I can get you some glue," Grace said. "I've got art class, so I'll bring it down here."

"If you can, that would be awesome," I said.

"I'll knock three times so you know it's not a teacher or anything," she said.

Taylor and Grace headed out the door, and I locked the door behind them.

The music room looked like a pretty good hideout. I hoped I didn't have any more reasons to hide, however, since the door was locked. I lay my skirt down and was examining it when suddenly the door opened.

!!!!! AHHHHHHHHHH! I was in my underwear!!!

I screamed, and so did the person walking into the room. I ducked behind a tuba. Please do not see me please do not see me . . .

"Hello?" the person said. At least it was female, considering I was half-dressed. I peeked over the top of the instrument and saw Arin Morgan. She was her usual stylish self in a white floaty top, jeans, and white wedge shoes.

"Um, I thought the door was locked," I said, standing up only just enough so my bottom half was blocked by the tuba. "You just freaked me out a little bit."

"Oh, Lynn!" she said. "Sorry, I have a key. There's usually never anyone in here! I didn't mean to scare you."

She walked in and put her tote bag down on the table next to my skirt.

"Is this a skirt you're making?" Arin said. "You really do get inspired; you just make clothes all the time, huh? No wonder you're the *GlITter Girl*. I'm sorry to startle you; I thought I was the only one who hid out here."

Arin hides out? From who? I was so surprised I stood up straight. Whoops.

"Um, do you know you're in your underwear?" Arin said.

There was no way out of it without seeming like even more of an idiot. I explained to her briefly what was happening.

"I'm sorry," she said, laughing. "It's just funny."

"I know," I said miserably. "Feel free to tell your friends. It will make a good story about the new IT Girl."

She waved me off. "Oh, I won't tell anyone. Especially if you don't tell anyone that I was in here. You know how it is in this school. I don't want everyone to find me here. Next thing you know, they'll all be here."

"I won't tell anyone," I said. Of course I was dying to ask her why she was hiding in the first place, but you just don't ask Arin Morgan that.

"You're probably wondering why I hide in here. I just need to get away from everything sometimes," she said. "I'm officially in study hall, but it's so noisy in there. Sometimes I need some peace and quiet."

She opened her tote bag and pulled out a fashion magazine.

"Oh yeah," she said, looking in her bag. "I have my cheerleading skirt if you want to wear that while you sew."

I was about to decline, when I realized that standing in my lime green frog underwear was not the best alternative. I put it on and twirled a little in it and then realized it looked ridiculous on me. "I've never worn a cheerleading skirt before. I'm not the cheerleading type like you are."

"Yeah," she said. "That's me, the cheerleading type."

I thought I detected some sarcasm in her tone, but she started reading her magazine, so I could have been wrong.

"Speaking of peace and quiet, look at this beautiful place." She held up her magazine.

I realized it wasn't a fashion magazine. It was a travel magazine.

"It's a remote island off South America." Arin sighed. "Wouldn't you love to go there?" I looked over her shoulder and saw a picture of a little hut and a river with a fishing boat. It wasn't what I was expecting. I pictured Arin as a spa and luxury hotel person.

"Aren't there times you just want to get out of here?" she said, closing the magazine. "I'd love to travel to places where I'm not Arin the cheerleader, and there are no preconceived notions about me. Don't you? Like, don't you love when you go to New York City and walk around and nobody's fazed by how you dress?"

"I wouldn't know." I shrugged. "I've never been to New York."

"You're kidding," Arin said. "What cities do you go to to get your style ideas?"

"None," I said. "Well, I went to Washington, D.C., once, but that's the only big city. And it's not exactly style central."

"That's even more amazing that you're so fashion forward," Arin said. "I just assumed you were so worldly."

"No, although my brother knows everything about every country," I said absentmindedly. "Not that we travel, but he does the Geography Bee for fun."

Oops. I don't know if Dex would appreciate me calling him Geography Bee boy to Arin Morgan.

"Really?" Arin said. "I should talk to him sometime."

Oh, Dex was so going to thank me for that. Suddenly there were three knocks at the door, and we both jumped.

"That's my friend Grace," I said. "She's bringing me glue."

Arin got up and opened the door.

"Hi, Jacob," Arin said. "Are you joining our party?"

I looked up and was surprised to see Jacob.

"Special glue delivery for Lynn Vincent," Jacob said, and held out a bottle of glue. "I'm in art class with a friend of yours, apparently. She got stuck being the teacher's assistant and asked me to sneak this to you. I'm officially in the bathroom again. Why do you need glue?"

"My skirt fell apart," I blurted out.

Arin snort-laughed.

"I mean . . . oh crud," I stammered. "I wasn't planning to share that."

Smooth. I felt my face burn.

"Like your sock fell apart at FonDo?" Jacob asked. "It's a little funny."

"My most embarrassing moments might be entertaining for you," I said, more testy than I meant to be. "But it was a fashion emergency."

"Whoa," Jacob said. "I didn't mean anything by it. You're embarrassed?"

"Well, hello," Arin piped up. "She just told you her skirt fell apart. That's embarrassing, Jacob."

"Mortifying," I said. "Sorry, I didn't mean to snap, but that was beyond embarrassing."

"Sorry," Jacob said. "You just always seem so chill, I thought you were along for the joke."

"Now you have to make her feel better," Arin said. "You need to confess something embarrassing so you're even."

"I knit," Jacob said. "That's not something I spread around."

"*You're* a knitter?" Arin and I said at the same time.

"Yeah, that's how I knew how to fix Lynn's sock thing," he said. "Even worse, I know how to embroider, too. My grandmother taught me. But you're both sworn to secrecy."

"Hmm," I said. "Okay, if you tell me one thing. How can I make better socks so they don't unravel?"

"Sounds like Jacob should give you knitting lessons, Lynn," Arin said.

An image flashed through my head of Jacob and me sitting together close, while he held my hands showing me how to knit, perhaps a nice blanket to cuddle under and—I blushed hard.

"Uh," I stammered, when my cell phone suddenly vibrated. "Oh, it's my phone."

"Lynn, this is Whitney from *GlITter Girl*," Whitney said when I answered. "I hope I'm not interrupting anything."

I shook my head to get the image of the cozy knitting lesson out of it.

"No, I'm good," I said.

"Lynn, we're getting such a positive response to the web page with the shoe," Whitney said. "One of our advertisers has asked to meet with you."

"Um, sure," I answered.

"It would require a short trip to their offices in New York City," Whitney said. "Your mother has given permission if you'd like to go. I wanted to call the advertiser back ASAP."

I leaned against the wall for support.

"Are you okay?" Arin whispered.

I muted the phone.

"Okay, you know how we were just talking about how I've never been to New York City?" I said, half in shock. "I'm going to New York City."

Catching up with our own IT Girl, Lynn:
A LYNN-terview

GGO: So first things first. How did your classmates

respond when they found out you were the first
IT Girl? I remember in your interview you said
they didn't "get you."

LYNN: Well, they were definitely surprised. Some
people probably think it's a weird choice.
I have gotten some compliments.

GGO: Well, we've heard nothing but compliments
about you. Our reader response has been
fabulous.

LYNN: Really? That's so cool!

GGO: What's also cool is we hear you're coming
to New York City tomorrow.

LYNN: Yes, I'm going to New York City tomorrow.
I'm so excited!! I'm packing right now.

GGO: We do know our IT Girl is going to take
NYC in style, there's no doubt. Stay tuned for
our next LYNN-terview!

I was in New York City. I couldn't believe that it had been
less than forty-eight hours since I'd been in the music
supply room discussing how I'd never been to New York
City. And now here I was riding in a white town car over
a bridge to Manhattan. I could see the Empire State Building, the skyline.

"I haven't been here in decades," my mom said, also
craning her neck. "Do I look like a tourist, or like someone
who knows what they're doing?"

"Someone who knows what they're doing, thanks to my
stylist-ness," I said. I'd helped her pick out her outfit and
had made her a fabulous glass beaded necklace.

I thought I looked pretty good, too. I felt like today
was a corporate-chic-meets-girl inspiration. I was wearing
a black-and-white houndstooth jacket that used to be my

mom's when she worked in an office. I'd completely deconstructed it and made it into a short jacket. I was extra happy with the gray with bright white pinstriped pants I was wearing. I'd added a red lining to the cuffs of the pants. I'd accessorized with a thick red pleather belt, a gold scarf for a little shine, and gold hoops. I wore my hair in a sleek ponytail swept to the side.

This was a dream come true. I looked out the window as we drove through the streets full of traffic. I saw brownstones and little stores and big stores.

I'd never seen so many people in my life walking through the streets, and they looked like they were from different places, backgrounds, and different fashion styles, too!

I tried to look up and out the windows to see the tops of the tall buildings. I saw signs for things I'd only seen on TV: Central Park, Madison Avenue, Fifth Avenue. I was longing to get out of the car and just soak it all up. But I was here for a meeting, so I had to put that feeling on hold.

"Are you nervous?" my mom asked me.

I genuinely wasn't. Whitney wouldn't be there, because *GlITter Girl* was in California, but she had reassured me I didn't have to give a speech or do anything scary.

"They just want to talk about what the shoe represents," she said. "And get some opinions about new directions for their company."

It was a company called Excelsiorama, Inc., which wanted to get more teen customers or something. I'd never heard of them, but if they were willing to fly me to New York for free, I was willing to talk!

"I'm not even a little nervous. There's no pressure," I said.

"Glad to hear it," my mom said. Then her cell phone rang. "There is one little surprise of the day. We're making a pit stop first."

And she handed me her phone.

"Hello, Lynn," a woman's voice said. "This is Valentyna. I hear you're in New York."

"Omigosh, I am!" I said. "I can't believe it. One of the *GlITter Girl* advertisers wants to meet me."

The car slowed down and pulled up to a sparkling building.

"They aren't the only ones who want to meet you while you're here," Valentyna said. "Look out your window. You have good timing, as my little Pasha needed a little outdoor visit."

I looked out the window. And standing there was a woman wearing a long dark coat and a silver-and-deep-emerald-green scarf around her head. Her dog was sniffing around the curb.

"Valentyna?" I gasped into the phone. The woman smiled, and the phone went silent.

"Surprise!" said my mom. "She wasn't sure if she'd be able to make it, so I didn't want to get your hopes up. And I didn't want you to get nervous."

"Okay, now I'm nervous," I said. Of course I'd seen Valentyna at the deli, but she'd never seen me. Of course I'd talked to her on the phone forever, sharing the whole shoe story. But here she was, in person. I was about to meet one of the most important fashion icons of our time. And she was about to meet *me*.

I took a deep breath and got out of the car. I stepped up the curb, and I was in front of Valentyna.

"Lynn." Valentyna leaned down and gave me an air kiss on both cheeks. "Welcome to New York. *J'adore* your whole look. And I must get a close-up look at those shoes."

"Thanks," I squeaked.

While my mom was saying hi and thanking her for everything, I petted Pasha and tried some deep-breathing techniques to stop myself from freaking out with excitement. Valentyna, the fashion icon, was standing here in front of me right now. Wait, apparently talking to my mother about . . . what?

"Lynn's tummy might be a little unsettled from the trip," my mom was saying. "And from all of this excitement. She may need to use the bathroom—"

"Um, Mom?" I interrupted, slightly horrified. "I'm fine. Really."

"Lynn!" Valentyna got the picture and turned to me. "We have a short amount of time together. We can see the sights, eat any kind of food you like, shop at the finest stores. My driver is here at our disposal. Lynn, what would you like to do?"

Thoughts raced through my mind, but there was really one thing I could do only with Valentyna, that I'd always wanted to: talk fashion with someone who gets it.

"Well," I said. "This might sound lame, but can we go somewhere and talk?"

"Not only is it not 'lame'"—Valentyna smiled and took my arm—"but I know exactly the place. I've seen your closet. Lynn, would you like to see my closet?"

"Omigosh," I breathed. "Yes."

Valentyna directed the driver to take my mom to the nearby art museum, and then Valentyna, Pasha, and I were walking up the steps to her place.

"I have worked in and owned many design studios all over the world," Valentyna told me. "But this studio is special to me."

!!!!

We walked into the building and into a large entry with an ivory-colored marble floor and cool art on the cream walls. Valentyna said hello to the doorman, and we got inside a small elevator.

"It's also special that this is your first time in New York," Valentyna said to me. "To me, New York is like a little slice of the world. The variety of people, of ideas, and of course the variety of fashions! And here is my little slice of New York."

The elevator doors opened, directly into—

"My personal studio," Valentyna said.

I gasped as I looked around at the studio. The floors were chocolate brown wood, set off by white trim. One wall was brick and the others a pale green, a shade between mint and olive. A huge window covered in white douppioni curtains let in a peek of sunlight and a view of the river. Vases full of white calla lilies made the room fragrant.

There were racks of clothes. And surrounding them

were baskets full of fabrics and bookshelves that held stacks of fabrics. The coffee table had fashion magazines on it, and in the center of the room was a large, well-used drafting table. I smiled when I saw a violet doggy bed in the corner that said PASHA. And there was even an inspiration wall, although Valentyna's was floor to ceiling. It was covered with photographs, sketches, torn-out magazine pages, and postcards.

"This is amazing," I gasped.

"Take a look around," Valentyna said. "And if you're like me and like to touch the fabrics, feel free."

I went over to the racks of clothes. I touched a deep gold dress and tried to imagine it on a model going down the runway in front of the fashion press, retail buyers, celebrities, and the entire who's who of the fashion world.

"As you know, Fashion Week introduces the two major seasons, spring and fall," Valentyna said. "That was part of a fall collection almost a decade ago. I have some of my favorite pieces archived here, though I occasionally let them out for museum retrospectives."

"They're gorgeous," I said. Then I pulled out an unusual one that looked like a cross between, well, bubble wrap and rubber tires.

"That dress was one of my showpieces," Valentyna laughed. "It was certainly vanguard, but I still love it. It definitely achieved the goal of getting attention for my runway show, but did get some criticism at the time."

"Doesn't that bother you?" I said.

"Fashion is fraught with criticism and rejection," Valentyna said. "You see it on a smaller scale from your peers. So if you face criticism from your classmates, just think of it as preparation for a future Fashion Week."

"I've been preparing for years, then." I grinned as I thought of the people who had made fun of my fashions.

"Many of us never quite fit in with the crowd," Valentyna said. "Being unique and original isn't always the key to high school popularity, but it can take you a long way in the fashion world. Standing out is easy in high school, but in fashion it's not so easy. Yet in fashion it's desirable. The key is to lead the trends, to make something that is distinctive."

I tried to memorize her words so I could keep them close to me on those days I could use them.

"Lynn, sometimes in fashion it seems like everything has been done, but there will always be fresh ideas. That's what we saw in you, and I want you to cherish that part of yourself."

"Wow. Thanks," I said genuinely.

Valentyna fell silent, and I walked around looking at all the amazing garments.

"I can't believe you did this by yourself," I said.

"Myself and my design assistants, sample makers, seamstresses, pattern makers. I could never do it without my production house." Valentyna laughed. "And businesspeople and publicists. It's a team effort."

"I could use seamstresses and help," I said. "I mean,

you saw my shoe and how it came unglued. And the other day I had a—let's just say, fashion emergency involving my skirt. But for now, it's just me designing alone in my closet, just for fun."

"It's been a long time since I designed a piece in here just for fun," Valentyna said wistfully. "Too long."

We both stood silently for a minute, and then Valentyna went over to one of the racks and pulled off a simple chocolate brown A-line dress.

"This is a dress I started but didn't have a vision for. Any thoughts?" Valentyna asked me.

"Well, it's close to the color of your gorgeous floors," I said. "It makes me feel inspired by your studio, with the brown floors and mint green and white flowers—"

"Well, shall we get to work?" Valentyna asked me.

"Definitely!" I said eagerly. "I'll be your pattern maker or hold the pins or whatever you want."

"Pshaw!" Valentyna said. "You'll be my partner. You've inspired me, thinking about *your* youthful energy. Not to mention for an inspiration wall of quotes from designers."

Valentyna looked at me.

"This must be a dress for you," she said. "We will resize and create."

And so I designed and created with fashion icon Valentyna.

Valentyna gave me advice on how to craft, how to balance proportions, how to sew more efficiently. But the design itself was a true collaboration.

We took skinny pieces of mint green ribbon and lay

the ribbon out to form words that I'd painted in my clos-et: CONFIDENCE * CREATIVITY * SELF-EXPRESSION * REACTION *

The ribbon circled the body of the dress at an angle. We handstitched the ribbon-words onto the dress, but Valentyna blocked off one center diagonal stripe.

"That is the spot for *your* signature word as well, Lynn," Valentyna said. "Express yourself front and center. You belong there among the designers now, Lynn."

"I don't have a word," I protested, and then realized I did.

I took some ribbon and made the word *Visible* on it.

I stood back and eyed the dress on the form. And I sighed with happiness.

"And that sigh of contentment means it's right," Valentyna said. "That was very satisfying. I think we made a fabulous team."

I almost passed out from joy. I couldn't stop grinning.

It was the best moment of my life. I closed my eyes and tried to capture the moment in my memory.

"After I made a new piece I used to take a picture to capture the memory," Valentyna said, apparently reading my thoughts. "Now of course I have fashion photographers take them who are much more talented than I am, but . . ."

Valentyna went over to a desk and picked up a large camera. "Let's see if this old thing still works." I stood next to the dress and she took the picture, which slid out of a slot in the camera.

"In the olden days we used these Polaroid instant cameras," Valentyna said. "You can watch the photo develop before your eyes. They no longer sell the film, so I save it for very special moments."

I watched as the picture got sharper and sharper, until it turned into me standing next to the dress. And both looking, if I do say so myself, fabulous. I pulled out my cell phone and took a picture of the picture.

"If you'd like, you may add that onto my design wall." Valentyna pointed to her wall. "Thumbtacks are on the desk."

"Seriously?" I said. I took the picture over to the wall and tried to figure out where to put it. I mean, I would definitely look out of place next to the supermodels wearing Valentyna on the runway, the celebrities wearing Valentyna on the red carpet—ah-ha! I found an empty spot right next to Pasha. I tacked myself up and smiled at the thought of being part of that glamorous group.

"I'll have the dress delivered to you at home so you don't have to carry it around," Valentyna said.

Just then, there was a loud buzzing sound.

"And speaking of deliveries . . ." Valentyna said cryptically, and left the room. When she came back, she was holding a long white box, which she handed to me.

"Go ahead and open it." She smiled.

I unwrapped it and dug through the tissue paper and pulled out—

"My shoe!" I gasped. It was my shoe! I held it up to see all the collaged pictures—there was me, Taylor, Bella, my creations. My little logo on the yellow sole.

"A long-deserved reunion," Valentyna said.

"I can't believe this started it all," I said. "I also can't believe the last time I saw it it was flying in the air toward your food, and I was running away in horror."

"We had to clean off a little raspberry vinaigrette dressing, but otherwise it's as good as new," Valentyna said.

"May *I* take a picture?" I asked her. I went to my bag and got my cell phone. I stood next to Valentyna and held up the shoe in one hand. I held out my phone and got a picture of us all together—me, Valentyna, and my shoe. Perfect.

nd then at the end, we took this picture." I held up
my cell phone to show my mom my new background
of me, Valentyna, and the shoe.

"I'm so glad you had a nice time," my mom said.

"Nice isn't even close to describing it," I said. "It was
epic."

I closed my eyes and leaned back against the black
leather seat of the car to revisit the experience. When I
was with Valentyna, I felt like I was almost a real designer, more than just Lynn. Like Taylor had said, I'd found
my people. I imagined myself as Valentyna's assistant—no,
partner—backstage at Fashion Week preparing our fall collection. The crowd would give us a standing ovation as our
model went down the runway, wearing the LynnDress and
of course, The Shoe. They'd be chanting, "Lynn! Lynn!"

"Lynn!" my mom repeated. "We're here."

I snapped out of it and looked out the window as the car pulled up in front of a black skyscraper. I took one last look at the picture on my cell and quickly sent it to Taylor. She'd be in the cafeteria right now, probably dying to hear how it was going. I knew she'd appreciate it. Then I climbed out of the car and followed my mom into a revolving door. I stood back and looked at the stark silver entryway as my mom signed us in with the doorman.

"Sixty-seventh floor," my mom said, pointing to an elevator.

"Whoa," I said. "That's pretty high."

We went into the empty elevator, which was mirrored on all sides. It started to move.

"Do I look okay?" I asked my mom. I put on some lip gloss and smoothed down my hair. "All of a sudden I'm nervous. I feel nauseous."

"That might be the elevator," my mom said. "Sixty-seven floors is pretty high up."

"I just realized something," I said. "What exactly is Excelsiorama, Inc.?"

"It's a company that owns smaller companies," my mom said. "When I Googled it, the list included small insurance companies and banks."

The elevator suddenly dipped and settled in. The doors slid open and we stepped out into a hallway. I followed my mom down the hall and into some offices. My mom went over to the receptionist, and I looked around. The walls had some framed prints of what looked like the company president shaking hands with the real president. There were framed awards for things like small business of the year.

"Pretty impressive," my mom said, checking them out.

"Welcome to Excelsiorama, Inc.!" A woman wearing a black suit and a deep red blouse with a subtle ruffle came out and shook my mom's hand and then held hers out to me. "I'm Irene, Senior Vice President of Marketing and New Development. And you must be Lynn."

"Hi," I said, shaking back firmly like I'd read somewhere you were supposed to do to impress businesspeople. "That color red is a great shade on you."

"She does have a good eye!" Irene said. "We have some people who are looking forward to hearing more about it."

We followed her down a hallway and into a room marked Executive Room. I walked in, and a group of businesspeople seated around a long table swiveled to look at us.

"Our guest of honor has arrived," Irene announced. "With her legal guardian."

Some of the people chuckled and smiled in my direction. It was like they were all checking me out, although in an interested way.

"Um, hi." I gave a little awkward wave. This was my first business meeting and I felt out of my league.

"Lynn, you can sit here," Irene said, pulling out a silver chair near the head of the table. It was the only seat without a gold-colored folder placed in front of it. I sat down.

My mom pulled up a chair next to me. Then people started introducing themselves. Somebody from advertising, someone from market research, someone from production. The names became a blur.

Irene quoted from one report that said teens spend close to 80 billion dollars a year on clothes, and footwear was performing well despite falling sales in other categories.

"Launching a footwear line makes sense for us," Irene explained. She went on to say how young women were becoming more and more fashion-forward, thanks to celebrity fashions, fashion magazines, and TV shows where even the private school uniforms were high-fashion.

Then a financial expert started talking about advertising numbers and gains and losses and I lost track of what they were talking about. I picked at some food that was on the table and tried to follow the discussion, but not successfully. The adrenaline rush I'd had at Valentyna's was starting to disappear. I actually started to wonder why my mom and I were even here.

"And that is why we are all here today: Lynn Vincent," Irene suddenly announced. She stood up and pointed right at me.

I sat up straighter, trying to look worth it.

Everybody clapped politely, and suddenly the businesspeople opened their folders.

"Please refer to page three in the packet," Irene said. "This is a full-color rendition of The Shoe. Lynn, we'd love to hear directly from you about how you created this shoe."

Everyone swiveled to look at me. Uh. Um. Okay. Just a little bit of pressure.

I took a sip of water and put my glass down on the table. Everyone at the table leaned in, including my mother.

I took a deep breath, and I told the story for what seemed like the millionth time. Although I'd never told it to a roomful of people wearing suits and taking notes. I told them how I created clothes and things that I thought were totally me. How I'd thought up The Shoe. And how it had been discovered by *GlITter Girl*. I left out the embarrassing parts, though, like the unraveling tights and kicking the shoe at Valentyna.

"Isn't she truly a gem?" Irene said, clapping again. Everyone at the table clapped along with her and muttered about what a gem I was.

I could feel my face turning red. But nobody could see it, fortunately, because the lights suddenly turned off and a PowerPoint presentation came on. Whew, hopefully I was done talking for a while. I blinked and watched the words come up on the screen.

TRENDS

"We've all discussed the buying power of the tween to teen market," Irene said, and her shadow showed up on part of the screen. "They have disposable income, even in today's economy. They respect both high fashion and personal do-it-yourself. Also known as DIY."

The PowerPoint clicked to the next slide.

INNOVATORS

"A new trend starts with the Innovators," Irene said.

"This is the first group to create and wear a new product."

INNOVATORS → EARLY ADOPTERS

Irene continued talking.

"After the Innovators start the trend, it moves to the Early Adopters. These are the girls on the *GlITter Girl* IT panel, the popular girls in the school. Once these trendsetters start wearing them, people will think they are cool."

INNOVATORS → EARLY ADOPTERS → MAJORITY

"Then the trend moves to the Majority. This constitutes most of the people who start wearing the trend after they've seen that it's cool. It's trickled down to the masses.

"Ladies and gentlemen," Irene said, somewhat dramatically. "As a company we've known we want to target the teen audience. But with *what,* we asked ourselves. And we have the answer."

Suddenly the PowerPoint slide that went up looked very familiar. It was the photo of me that was on the *GlITter Girl* site.

"We have the Innovator we need," she said. "Lynn Vincent."

I'm the Innovator? I mean, I create things in my closet, duh. But, hello? It's not like I really wear something and people, as she called it, Early Adopt it. Much less the masses.

I looked at my mom, and she gave me a little shrug. We just sat and listened to Irene.

"We wanted to find the Innovators for our new product launch, which will be picked up by the Early Adopters and then trickle down to the Majority.

"And we've found a true Innovator: Lynn. Lynn is organic. She is a visionary straight from the street. And that, ladies and gentlemen, is why we have found the first shoe that Excelsiorama, Inc., wants to launch.

"Just imagine, people, this shoe is the first in a new line of groundbreaking, trendsetting shoes specifically for teen girls. Move over, Manolo; step aside, Louboutin; swish off, Nike. Just imagine the new launch: Lynn's Shoe."

The PowerPoint clicked to a new screen showing a shoe. *My* shoe.

It hit me then. What if my shoe was sold in stores? The shoe that I'd made in my closet all by myself and loved, and caused what I thought to be one of the worst moments of my life? What if I went into a store and there was a shelf of shoes, designed by me, Lynn Vincent? Lynn Vincent, former—kind of still—freak?

What if people actually bought my shoes? And wore them?

!!!!!!!!!!!!!!!!!!!!

can't believe they might carry your shoe in stores!!!"
Taylor whisper-screamed. We were in the backseat of
her mother's SUV, getting a ride to school.

"Shh!" I said. I pointed to her mother, who was trying
to look like she wasn't listening. But I knew she was, and
ready to spill everything while she worked out at her country club after dropping us off.

I'd gotten in really late last night, but I'd texted Taylor
the summary: The Excelsiorama, Inc., people wanted to
buy my shoe design. I'd get paid; I'd be the designer; and
they'd make and market my shoe.

"It's still confidential, so don't tell anyone," I said.

"I won't," Taylor promised. "It's just so exciting."

"Well, don't get too excited yet," I said. "I didn't really
understand all the business part of it. My mom is getting a
lawyer to help us figure it all out."

After the big announcement I was kind of in shock and pretty much missed the rest of the presentation. Manufacturers, distributors, pricing. I caught the drift but was overwhelmed with the details. I did appreciate everyone gushing about the shoe, but it was overshadowed by the thought of my shoe in actual stores. My brain was fried by the time my mom told them we'd talk further. The town car had picked us up and whisked us back to the airport, and we'd flown home.

Now I was heading back to school as if everything were normal. Although earlier than usual, because Taylor said she had an early-morning meeting for something. And with her mother being nicer, even bringing me a chai from the coffee place.

"This is so freaking cool," Taylor said. "Can you imagine if your shoe was sold in stores? I bet you could make a ton of money."

I can't say I hadn't thought about that part! I can't say Dex hadn't either when I came home and told him about what had happened. He'd gotten out his über-calculator and was still running numbers when I fell asleep, exhausted.

"It all doesn't seem real," I told her. "That was only part of the day. I have to tell you about Valentyna, too."

"That picture was sweet," Taylor said. "If anyone gives you a hard time today, you just flash that picture on your cell phone. 'What did *you* do yesterday? *I* was hanging out with Valentyna, famous fashion designer.' Ha! I hope Chasey gives you some snotty—"

"Taylor, are you telling Lynn about Chasey?" Mrs. Snyder suddenly called out from the front seat. "Did you tell her the good news?"

"Sorry I hogged the whole conversation. What's your good news?" I turned to Taylor.

"Chasey Welch called Taylor last night!" Mrs. Snyder trilled. "She invited her to be on the school social committee."

"Oh, did she?" I said.

"You girls will have so much fun," Mrs. Snyder said.

"You *girls,* plural?" I whispered. "I hope that means you and Chasey? I'm not on a social committee, am I?"

Fortunately, Taylor shook her head no.

"Phew," I said.

Mrs. Snyder was still chatting away. "Taylor, tell Lynn what you and Chasey were planning."

"Well, the social committee is going to have a fundraiser," Taylor said. "I suggested that it be for a charity, this children's rec center."

"That's a great idea, Taylor," I said. "Isn't it, Mrs. Snyder? Isn't Taylor *so nice* for thinking of a charity?"

There. That would have to make her mom proud. However, I'd underestimated her mother.

"Oh, that wasn't the exciting part," her mother said. "Taylor, tell Lynn about the fashion show."

"Um," Taylor said, squirming.

"A fashion show is a good idea," I said carefully. I looked at Taylor and she didn't look at me.

"Ooh! How about a *mother-daughter* fashion show?" her

mother said. "Taylor! You can suggest that to Chasey."

"No!" Taylor and I both blurted out, horrified. Fortunately the car pulled up to the curb before she could continue that line of thinking.

"Oh, too bad we're here already," I said, trying to sound sincere as I got out of the car. "Thanks for the ride, Mrs. Snyder!"

I hopped out, careful not to spill my chai.

"What are you not telling me?" I asked her.

"A mother-daughter fashion show would be a *nightmare*," Taylor said. "But a regular fashion show could be kinda fun? I mean a little, right?"

"Sure, you could have fun with that," I said. "You and your social committee."

"Please don't kill me," Taylor said. "I kind of said you would, you know, help out a little."

"I thought you said I'm not on the social committee!" I said.

"I did! You're not!" Taylor said, and then her words spilled out in a rush. "You're just on the fashion show. They want you to do a fashion show of your creations."

She cringed and looked for my reaction.

"Tay, I really don't want to do a school fashion show," I said. "You know that."

"Chasey's in charge of it," Taylor said. "She called my *mother*. She told my mother she wanted me on her social committee to run it with her. Of course my mother was like falling all over herself to tell her yes."

"Taylor," I groaned.

"I had no choice," Taylor wailed. "We both know the only reason Chasey asked me was so that I could get you to help with the fashion show. Chasey knows you wouldn't say yes to her. So yes, I'm being used to get to you."

"Tay, do you even want to do this?" I asked her. She nodded.

"You saw my mother," Taylor said. "She's all excited and proud of me for once. I can just do this and make her happy forever. And raising money for charity is a good cause, right?"

"Yes," I sighed. "And I'll do it for another good cause. You."

"You'll help?" Taylor squealed and threw her arms around me. "Thank you! Thank you! Okay! Okay! I'm going to leave now before you change your mind. Thanks, Lynn!"

Taylor bounced up the stairs as I trudged alongside her. Great. What did I just agree to? I trudged into school. So, now I would be helping Chasey and company with the school fashion show. Just a few weeks ago, I was standing at my locker and people were making fun of my clothes. Now they were calling it a fashion show.

Just yesterday, I was in New York City. With Valentyna. And being offered a possible shoe line.

Things were changing so fast around here, my head was spinning. Well, now I had a half hour to kill before school started. I went up to my locker and put my stuff away.

One of the pom-poms on my ironic-cute mirrors was peeling off, so I took out some glue from my emergency kit and stuck it back on. I caught a glimpse of myself in the mirror; I looked seriously tired. I'd barely gotten any sleep and barely any study time. It was really quiet and I had the hall to myself, so I might as well study for my math quiz. I sat down on the floor, put my chai next to me, and leaned against the locker.

If $12z - 16 = 20z$ then what is z?

What is z?

Z?

Zzzzz.

"Lynn? Lynn?"

I opened my eyes to see Jacob leaning over me. He looked quite cute in a bright blue polo over a long-sleeve white shirt, dark skinny jeans, and the sneakers I liked. Okay, wait, huh? Where was I? I must have fallen asleep sitting at my locker. Well, this was embarrassing.

"Are you here early, too?" I asked. Please tell me that school hadn't started and a thousand people hadn't walked by and pointed at me asleep on the floor.

"Yeah, I have a group project meeting," Jacob said. "Were you asleep just now?

"Um, no!" I said. "Just um, thinking."

"Cool, about what you're going to design next?" he said. "You're pretty focused."

I was fully awake now, and realizing that I was pretty much sprawled out on the floor. I picked up my math book and tried to get up off the floor and redeem my dignity.

I say "tried to" because I was immediately yanked back. My head was not getting up. I felt the back of my head. It felt sticky. Stuck, like glue. Oh no, I had used glue trying to fix my locker. I must have gotten glue on my hands and then smoothed my hair down and . . . glued my head to my locker. I had glued my head to my locker.

"Maybe you can teach me to focus like that," Jacob said, sliding down until he was sitting next to me. "I've got a killer social studies test today and nothing is sticking in my brain."

"Mmm-hmm," I said. I pulled my hand up to my hair and tried to unstick myself. Ow. I was yanking little hairs out of my skull. Ow.

"I really admire that about you," he continued, looking at me with those big dark eyes that crinkled when he smiled. "You're so passionate. About your clothes, I mean."

And I admire how he thinks I'm admirable. And did he just say passionate? I tried to squirm a little to unstick my hair. I accidentally pulled so hard I practically fell on top of him. I was about to be totally embarrassed and apologize, but he smiled. And Jacob leaned toward me and his head tilted a little and his face moved close to mine. He was leaning very close to me. Very close.

Uh.

Uh. I leaned, too, not sure what was happening. He pulled me forward a little, and—

Ouch! Too far forward! It yanked my hair stuck to the locker! I grimaced and whipped my head back toward the locker, away from Jacob. Jacob jumped back, too.

"I just—I—" I sputtered. Oh forget it. I couldn't even begin to explain what had just happened.

"Well!" Jacob stood up awkwardly. "I better get to class. You can go back to your focusing."

I sat there as he gathered up his books and said a quick good-bye. I sat there as he went off down the hall. Okay. What had just happened? Maybe I was just imagining the whole thing. But I swear for a second there was going to be a . . .

A kiss!

No, I must have imagined that in my tired delirium. I leaned my stuck head back against the locker. Kissing at the lockers was for the Makeout Couple, who, by the way, were walking toward me. Oh great. Please let them start their session at least a few lockers down from me, since I wasn't going to be able to move.

The girl half of Makeout Couple detached her hand from her boyfriend's back pocket and came over to me.

"Hi, Lynn," the girl half of Makeout Couple said, looking down. "I was so inspired by your iron-on T-shirt thing the other day, I made matching T-shirts for me and my sweetie. Honey, come show her the shirt."

Makeout Guy came over. They unzipped their jackets and showed me their matching shirts with each other's pictures ironed on. Hers said I LUV HIM. His said I LUV HER.

Uh. I apparently was inspiring some . . . interesting things.

"You said to wear what made us feel good," she said. "And what makes me feel good is my honey-boo." She wrapped her arms around him and started nibbling on his ear. That was a very sweet sentiment. And still way too much PDA. I tried to get up to move away, but I'd forgotten I couldn't.

"Ow!" I said as my head got yanked back again.

Makeout Guy started cracking up.

"Dude, your head is glued to the locker, isn't it?" he said. "I remember when the football team glued this guy's head to the team bus window when he fell asleep. It was hilarious until he woke up and ripped out some of his hair."

"Oh, great," I said, feeling panicky.

"Who did that to *you*?" he said. "You don't play football, do you?"

"I did it to myself," I said. "And I can't get free."

"Coach made us set the guy free by pouring warm water on his head," he said. "Hey, is that a warm drink? I can try that."

He picked up my chai, and before I knew what he was doing he poured it on the back of my head.

"Honey! You can't pour a drink on the IT Girl!" Makeout Girl half-screamed.

"No, wait," I said. I moved my head around. "I think it's working."

I pulled my hair slowly off the locker. I was free!

"It worked!" I said. "Hey, thanks!"

"Honey, you're a genius!" gushed Makeout Girl. She wrapped her arms around him and the makeout session began. At least this time I could move away from the action.

I was free, but I was also now wet and slimy. And probably smelly.

And when I thought of Jacob, I was definitely confused.

It only got more confusing after I ran into Jacob again at our lockers.

"Hi," I said, shifting slightly to the other side to ensure I wasn't close enough for him to smell chai or notice my hair was matted. Or that I was blushing, thinking about our almost-close encounter.

"Hey, Lynn." He turned to open his locker.

I waited, but he didn't say anything else. So obviously, I'd been delusional thinking we'd had a moment, or if we had he obviously had come to his senses since. I was trying to think of something to say, but two girls came up to him whom I recognized as Popular People. I stuck my head in my locker to avoid him avoiding me.

"Jacob, do you want to work on the group project after FonDo?" the one with long black hair asked.

I tried not to look like I was spying, although I kind of was, but the other girl leaned over to me.

"Jacob and Megan were such a cute couple," she sighed. "They broke up last year, but maybe they'll get back together someday."

I couldn't help but agree with her on the first one. They would have made a cute couple. I didn't think people would think that about me and Jacob. He was normal and I was . . . different. I mean, really, we couldn't even begin to look like a couple by anyone's stretch of the imagination. We would be a weird style mash-up. I was kind of mad at myself for even going there in my imagination.

I shut my locker door and walked down the hall without looking back. I just needed to go to class and focus. I had a quiz to make up. I needed to put all of this craziness out of my head. And then suddenly, a random girl jumped in front of me.

"What do you think?" she asked me as she twirled around in front of me. She was wearing tall black boots, dark denim shorts, black tights, and a black-and-white striped shirt with a slouchy gray cardigan over it. It looked suspiciously like what I'd worn last week, except my tights had been mustard on one leg and black on the other.

"I saw it on LikeLynn," she said.

"Like what?"

"The website? LikeLynn? Mostly I like LynnIsIT better, but I don't know where to find some of that stuff. Like I couldn't find the yellow-and-black tights."

I backed slowly away.

"You don't like it," she said, worried. "I'm sorry, I couldn't find the right tights. I tried, though!"

"That's not it," I said. "You look good. I . . . gotta go."

I quickly went off down the hall to my locker. Like-Lynn? LynnIsIT? Things were getting really strange. I turned the corner and practically ran into Grace.

"Welcome back!" she said. "I can't wait to hear about New York."

"Hey," I said. "I can't wait to tell you. But first, do you have two minutes and your iPhone with you?"

"Sure." She pulled her phone out of her bag.

She handed it to me and I Googled LikeLynn. It was a site with the slogan "A website where you can be exactly like the IT Girl."

"You're kind of pale," Grace said.

"I just discovered an alternate universe," I told her. "There are websites about me."

"Oh. I take it Taylor didn't tell you?" Grace asked me.

I shook my head and scrolled through and saw it had been started two days ago. It had pictures of clothes I had never worn, but the blogger apparently thought were my style. And then I pulled up the website called LynnIsIT.

I scrolled through.

"Aw, this is nice." I smiled. "It says I'm a celebration of all that is unique and empowering about girls."

"Oh, good," Grace blurted. "I thought you meant the other ones."

"What other ones?" I asked her, and her face dropped.

"Um," she said. "Nothing. Can I have my phone back?"

Oh boy. I quickly Googled myself. Oh. There *were* other ones. And let's just say, people weren't always nice.

After I read aloud the blog entry that said I was hideous with no sense of style *and* needed a pimple cream, Grace had taken her phone from me and forced me to go to my class. Where, of course, I bombed the quiz, since all I could think about was blogs dissing me. And Jacob not kissing me.

After class, Taylor met me at my locker.

"I got Dex to give us a ride to your house," Taylor told me. "I'm coming over."

"I'm okay," I said. "You don't have to babysit me."

"Yes, we do. I know you're going home to read those blogs," Taylor said. "And we're going to block you from your computer, Lynn."

I waited an extra minute just in case Jacob went to his locker. But when he didn't, I walked with Taylor outside to the parking lot. Dex was waiting for us with my mom's car.

"You know all celebrities have haters," Taylor said reassuringly. "It's the price you pay for celebritiness. Ignore it. Try not think about it."

"I know," I said. "I mean, if I really cared what people said about my clothes I wouldn't wear these clothes to begin with."

I always had people saying things about me. It went

along with wearing my creations. But that was at least limited to school, or people who saw me. Being online was kind of weird.

"It's not like I'm making people wear my style," I muttered. "I want people to have their own style."

"We really should tell the principal about that one blog," Taylor said "You could practically see the school name on the wall. I think that's an invasion of privacy."

"What?" I asked her.

"Oh," Taylor said carefully. "Didn't you see the blog with the pictures of you in the school hallways?"

"What?!" I shrieked. "No! Who's doing that?"

"Don't worry, they cut off your head," Dex said cheerfully. "It's just one big critique of your outfits."

"That's creepy," I said. "I didn't know I had a stalker. I thought it was weird enough that some people were imitating my clothes."

"I know I'm supposed to feel sorry and supportive of you here," Taylor said. "But I'm also jealous you have stalkers and imitators."

"Sorry," I said. "I'm sure you will."

"I did try to be the first one to 'incorporate three key pieces in this winter's hottest colors.' That's according to one of my fashion blogs. Did it work?" Taylor pointed at her outfit. She wore a bulky oversize sweater belted over a vest and a chunky scarf.

"Well, yes," I said. "But isn't it a little warm out for that?"

"Heck, yeah. I can't stand it anymore. I'm taking off two of the three key pieces," she said. "I was sweating to death all day. I thought I was going to pass out." She pulled off her sweater, vest, and scarf, revealing a cute red-and-white T-shirt that said COMMUNITY REC CENTER with stick figure kids across the front and VOLUNTEER on the back.

"You could have just stuck with the tee," I said. "It's cute. Did you volunteer for something?"

"Oh, kinda. Anyway, more importantly, I was trying to be the first with the three key pieces in next season's hottest color trend." Taylor sighed. "I'm not giving up on this. Someday, somehow, I will connect with fashion. Without relying on you, Miss IT."

"I'm sure you can find your own style," I reassured her.

"Speaking of style." Dex cleared his throat and said, "Uh, I hear Arin Morgan is doing a fashion show with you guys."

Taylor elbowed me and grinned.

"How did you hear that?" I asked smoothly.

"She told me in chemistry class," he said.

"Oooh, so you're talking to Arin now?" I said. "Are you making chemistry in class?"

"Shut up. Or else you can just ride the bus." Dex glared in the rearview mirror. "Or with Taylor's mother."

"We'll be nice," Taylor said quickly. "Yeah, Arin is one of the models."

"Well, uh, you know if she comes over to get her clothes or whatever," Dex muttered, "let me know."

"I will, I promise," I said. "I hope *I* get to meet them."

Most of the models were going to be from the IT panel, but I didn't know who they were yet. Chasey said Arin was, of course, going to be one, but she was going to choose the others and let me know.

"She told me just to get started and design the best fashions," I said. "But I'm trying to convince her I need to see the models so the fashions can really represent them."

Valentyna had told me she likes how I try to make my creations bring out the best in the people who are wearing them. I loved that. I envisioned my first fashion show like that, me bringing out the best in each model.

"Dex, maybe you can ask Arin when she can come over for a fitting after school."

"Sure!" Dex said cheerfully. "No problem."

"You made his day," Taylor whispered to me as the car pulled into our driveway.

As I got out of the car, I was surprised to see my mom come out the front door. She held up the phone and waved to me.

"Lynn has a business call. It's Irene from Excelsiorama," my mom said, handing the phone to me. "It's good news. Taylor, why don't you come in and have a snack? I picked up some fondue when I picked up Dex's paycheck for him."

"Anything but fondue," Dex groaned. "It's my day off."

"Good luck," Taylor said to me, and followed Dex inside.

I took the phone and stood on the front porch.

"Hello?" I said.

"Lynn, sweetie," Irene said. "We have some exciting news for you. Our investors agreed and we're going to test-market your shoe as the kickoff to our new line. If the line tests well, which we believe it will, your shoe will be advertised and sold everywhere."

"Wow," I said, and sat down on the step. Wow. It could be really happening. My shoe could really be sold in stores.

"So with your permission—we discussed the details with your mother—we're going to start the process by having a few people test the shoe."

"They're going to wear my shoe?" I asked. "Do you need me to design something?"

"For now, they will just try a prototype of a shoe similar to yours and give us some feedback. Just say yes and an initial check will be in the mail."

"Um," I said. "I should probably talk to my mom before I say yes."

"I'll hold," Irene said cheerfully. "But not too long. We've already manufactured prototypes of your shoe. Just think, fifty copies will be overnighted and worn on our test models within days!"

I thanked her and went inside. Mom was sitting at the kitchen table with Taylor.

"What should I do?" I asked my mom.

"Well," she said. "It's not a full commitment, so we could see how it goes. It's a nice amount of money to go into your savings, too."

I nodded and handed her the phone. My mom stood up and left to talk to Irene.

"Whoa," Taylor said, after I explained what just happened. "That would be huge. Can you imagine walking into a store to buy shoes and seeing yours on the shelf? And then walking into school and seeing everyone wearing your shoe?"

"It's kind of weird, though, because the shoe was so personal to me. I don't exactly get how they're going to make it for everyone. I mean, there are pictures of you and me on the shoe," I said. "I wonder if they'll have a site where you upload your own pictures to go on the shoe."

"That would be sweet," Taylor said.

"I can make you a pair," I said.

"Oh, you don't have to do that," Taylor protested. "They're *your* special shoe. Well, until they're mass-produced by that company."

"You're just worried I won't glue them right and you'll trip and they'll fly off into someone's plate," I said.

"No!" Taylor protested. "Well, maybe."

"Gee, thanks," I laughed. "Well, don't get too excited anyway. The test people could hate them, just like those haters on the Internet. Which reminds me, I need to brace myself and go read those blogs to see what people are saying about me."

"Oh, just read the nice ones," Taylor said. "Besides, it's not like anyone can take a blog that spells *loser* wrong seriously."

What did I get myself into?

"Someone called me a loser? It's going to be hard to not take this personally," I said.

"Lynn, remember how on the first day of school you said you had to be yourself even if people were going to make fun of you or give you weird looks?" Taylor said.

"I meant in school. I didn't mean online all over the country," I grumbled.

"Well, when one of the bloggers gets chosen to be the next *GllTter Girl* IT Girl, hang out with Valentyna in New York, and have their shoe sold in stores, then you can worry about it. Okay?" Taylor asked me.

"Thanks," I said to her. "That actually helps."

It had been a weird couple of days which I'd pretty much spent convincing myself not to look at the meaner blog comments and then reading the meaner blog comments. Today I was wearing an outfit that I could feel thick-skinned in. Literally. I wore a thrifted pleather vest for a feeling of toughness with a bleached-out denim skirt. Shredded black tights and motorcycle boots for Don't mess with me. And a white T-shirt with a peace sign I'd hand-painted with some old puffy paint, to show that I came in peace, despite the bloggers who wanted to battle against me. Top it all off with a black-bow headband and there I was today.

"Hi, Lynn." A girl walked past me down the hall wearing a black-bow headband.

Then a girl wearing shredded black tights. This was an awfully strange coincidence. Before I had time to process, my brother came up to me. He was wearing a charcoal gray shirt I'd made last night as a thank-you for driving me home. I had bleached a pattern on it, using leftover bleach from my denim skirt. It had turned out quite good, if I do say so myself.

"Hey," he said. "Mom said she's going to be late tonight."

Before I could answer, a girl walked past us. She was wearing a white T-shirt with a peace sign like mine, but apparently drawn on with marker.

"Hi, Lynn!" she called out. "Ooh, Dex! Your shirt is even cooler in person!"

"It did turn out cool, if I do say so myself," I told him. Then I paused. "Wait a minute. Why did she just say it was cuter in person? Where else could she have seen it?"

"I liked it so much I put a pic of it on my Facebook last night," Dex said.

"And she was wearing a peace sign on her shirt like me? And this girl was wearing a black bow like I am and another pair of shredded black tights? Do you know anything about that?"

"Oh," Dex said. "I didn't know people would steal your ideas. They just asked me what you were going to wear, and when I went in to ask you, your clothes were hanging up, so I took a picture."

"Dex!" I said. "You can't tell people what I'm going to wear! It's invading my privacy . . . or my originality . . . or something."

"You're right. I'm sorry," he said. "I just walked in and

then, well, you know. Cute girls asking me for things. I choked."

"You're selling me out to flirt with cute girls?" I asked him.

"Er, I guess," he said. "I won't do it again. But shouldn't you feel flattered they want to copy you?"

"I'm on an emotional roller coaster," I told him. "This is all very confusing. People are copying me in school. People are debating if I'm a poseur or a talentless freak on blogs."

"Well, if you need me to kick someone's butt, let me know," Dex said. "I mean, Dex-style. I could hack into their blogs and take them down."

"Thanks, but I'm okay," I said. "See you later."

And I *was* okay for approximately three seconds. Because then I turned the corner and saw something walking down the hallway that really threw me off guard. Chasey looked her usual gorgeous self, in a designer jacket, jeans, and . . .

My shoe.

MY SHOE. Well, actually both shoes were my shoe.

"Surprise!" She held up her foot. "They only selected a few of us on the IT panel to get the prototypes, and I was chosen!"

I was temporarily speechless. I leaned over to look at it and saw Bella's little face staring back at me. And pictures of my creations. And a little picture of me and Taylor.

"I'll let you know how the shoes work out for me," Chasey said. And with the proverbial toss of her hair, she continued down the hall.

I continued to be speechless, until someone tapped me on the shoulder.

"Lynn, are you okay?"

I turned around to see Grace, looking concerned. She steered me off to the side of the hallway and leaned me against a locker.

"Not really," I said. "I've just had the surreal experience of seeing Chasey wear a mock-up of my shoe that she is testing for the IT panel."

"That *is* awkward," Grace said. "I mean, that shoe is so personal to you."

"I mean I knew it would happen once I told Excelsiorama they could test it out," I said. "And then it could be sold in stores everywhere. But I thought it would be different. I thought they'd put their own pictures on it, but there was my dog, my inspiration board, my creations out there for just anyone to see. And I never thought I'd see it on Chasey's foot. Ew. Chasey."

"That's very weird," Grace said. "But think of it this way—a couple weeks ago if I told you Chasey Welch would be wearing—and showing off—one of your creations, what would you have thought?",

"I never would have believed it," I said. "But true, I would have felt slightly validated. Thanks, you're cheering me up."

"But wait, what if I'd said she'd be wearing your face on it?" Grace asked.

"Chasey wearing my picture is kind of ironic, isn't it?" I said, smiling a little. And then I started smiling wide as I realized something else. "And Chasey is wearing Taylor's face proudly, too. That makes it seem a little more worthwhile."

So I decided to celebrate my fresh take on the situation and good mood by meeting Taylor and Grace at FonDo. And on the way back to "our" table area, I made a point of accidentally on purpose bumping into Chasey. This time I was prepared.

"Hi, Chasey," I said confidently, getting the attention of the boothful of people she was sitting with.

Taylor looked at me, like what was I doing? I smiled at her.

"Chasey, I just wanted to say how cool it was you got to be one of the first people to wear the shoe."

"I know," she sighed. "It's so awesome being on the IT panel and getting things before the rest of the world."

"May I take a picture of you wearing the shoe?" I asked her, holding up my phone.

"Of course," she said. I shot one of her posing, and then a close-up of her shoe.

"Taylor," I said, turning to her. "How funny is it that Chasey is wearing your face on the shoe? I'm so glad I put you on there."

"Oh, yeah," Kayden said, leaning under the table to see. "Look, Taylor's like a Chanel logo or something."

"Let me get a picture of you two together," I said. Chasey had no choice but to smile and say cheese. Taylor's beaming smile was less forced.

"Okay, that was sweet," Taylor said as we walked back

to our table. "I've never been compared to a designer logo before."

"That made Chasey wearing my shoe much easier to take," I said, and slid into a chair next to Grace. Plus I was going to forward those pictures to Taylor's mother.

"Hi!" Grace said. "You guys look happy."

"It's the little things that make me happy," Taylor said. "Like harmless revenge. And also fondue."

"I can serve up both for you." My brother came up and took out his order pad. We ordered and then my phone rang.

"You guys, I have a message from Excelsiorama, Inc., that my mom forwarded," I said.

Lynn, we have had a tremendously positive response to your shoe. Thus, we will be making a formal offer to sell your shoes in stores. We will be in touch. In the meantime, please enjoy the following sample campaign our advertising staff put together.

I looked up at Taylor, Grace, and Dex.

"It's official! They're going to make my shoe," I announced, and tried to process it as reality as Grace and Taylor squealed and hugged me. Even Dex high-fived me.

"If they can work out a deal with my mom and everything," I added. "She told me we're not going to do anything I'm not comfortable with."

"Of course she'll work out a deal," Dex said. "She's already planning on using your profits to send you to college.

She figures you're going to go to New York City to fashion school, so it's going to be expensive. And your grades aren't that great, so you won't get a scholarship."

"She said that?" I asked him.

"Yeah, on the phone to Aunt Jen," Dex said. "She was pretty pumped up. I mean, she is a single mother, so this will help the financial pressure."

Well, I was glad to be helpful.

"They sent me a link to show me their advertising campaign." I held up my phone. "But I can't get the Internet."

Grace pulled out her iPhone and started setting it up. "Got it."

"This is so exciting," Taylor said as a little tape started playing.

First, there was some music.

Dex snorted. "Cheesy music."

"Shush!" Taylor smacked his arm. "Or go away."

"He's right, though," I said. "It's painful. Hopefully it's just a place holder."

Then suddenly a picture of my shoe appeared on the screen. And the words underneath them read:

Introducing SHEWZ! For Phab Pheet That Phunk!
Uh.

We all sat there and stared at the screen, even though it had gone black. Dex's snort broke the silence.

"Well!" Taylor said, brightly. "That was . . ."

"Phab Pheet That Phunk?" Dex laughed. "What's up with that?"

"And Shewz?" I said. "That's kind of . . ."

"Cheesy? Lame? Ridiculous?" Dex said, but shut up when Taylor gave him a dirty look.

"What does Phunk mean?" Grace asked tentatively.

"I have no idea," I said. "But it sounds awkward. It sounds like smelly feet. That's not the slogan I was hoping for."

"Well, that's what you get for selling out!" Dex said cheerfully.

I didn't want to sell out, obviously. I did want college savings. I did want to see my shoes in the store. But phab pheet that phunk obviously . . . stunk.

"You don't have to do anything you're not comfortable with," Taylor said. "Remember, I'm quoting your mom."

"Yeah, well, my mom would like the college tuition money, I'm sure." I sighed. "And come on, when else am I going to get my shoes made and sold in stores? It's a huge opportunity and we all know it."

"Lynn." Taylor looked at me. "You can say no to Shewz."

And then Chasey grabbed a chair from Char's table and scooted it over.

"Omigosh," she said. "You guys are the best ever. Taylor, I just know I was brilliant having you on the social committee. The whole Shewz thing, it's going to make this the best fashion show."

And Chasey leaned over and gave me a hug. And Taylor a hug. Taylor looked as confused as I felt. Grace stepped in to clarify things.

"What's the whole Shewz thing?" Grace asked.

"Well! This company Excelsiorama that owns Shewz

and gave me the shoes to test out is going to sponsor our fashion show," Chasey said. "Once they found out about Lynn's connection to me and the IT panel, they were really into it. Cash donation."

"That's awesome!" Taylor said. "We already have a donation for charity!"

"And that's not even the best part," Chasey said. "The Shewz people told the IT panel they're trying to discover their next model for their advertising campaign. They're going to pick one of their models from our show!"

"Really? That's awesome," I said.

"But more difficult for me." Chasey sighed dramatically. "The girls on the IT panel are just going crazy begging me to choose them."

"Well, can you please choose them quickly?" I asked her. "I'm going crazy planning the outfits."

"I'll let you know," Chasey said. And she floated off to the front of the room.

"Okay, so that was kind of good news, bad news right?" Taylor ventured hopefully. "Emphasis on the good news."

"Great news about the sponsor for charity," I muttered. "But added pressure if Excelsiorama, Inc.—or should I say Shewz?—is coming to my first fashion show. I don't even have models! Why can't Chasey just choose?"

I got my answer when I overheard Kayden and Kyla waiting in line for the girls' room.

"Just because we're not on the IT panel doesn't mean Chasey can't pick us to model," Kayden whined.

"They're all sucking up to her so bad," Kyla complained.

"One girl is taking Chasey for a spa day. Another one bought her a new bag!"

Oh. Chasey was getting bribed. And I'm sure she was enjoying the power trip as Queen Bee of the IT panel. My cell phone buzzed with a message from Chasey.

> Forgot to tell u! Our fashion show has a new slogan too: Phab Phunky Phashion Show!
> Chasey

"Phab Phunky Phashion Show?" I groaned and held out the cell phone for Taylor and Grace to see. "Is it just me or is this all going wrong?"

Taylor and Grace looked at each other, but didn't say anything. I knew. It phunked.

Designers have themes for their fashion shows. Flowers, decades, romantic elegance, rockers, superheroes. Even insects.

I'd chosen my theme: school. Okay, I know it seems kind of boring. But I wanted to express what my models and audience were really going through and since 80 percent of our adolescence is wasted—I mean spent—in high school, it actually was the ideal theme. And, of course, me being me, it wasn't going to be normal high school. I was going to take school style to the next level.

I would start with the first-day-of-school outfit, the First Impressions outfit. I'd cycle all the way through to the last day of school.

I pulled the prom dress I'd made off the hanger to admire it. It was a sophisticated navy blue, off-the-shoulder with beaded detailing on the front. The navy blue faded as it got to the bottom, and underneath was a smoky gray that you could see as the full skirt swirled. I wanted it to look like the fabric was dancing as the model walked. And the back had a semi-low V to add interest. It was going to look stunning on Arin Morgan. It was going to be the final piece for the show and finish off my theme.

And Chasey finally picked the models. I sketched, found fabrics, got the clothes ready. It was two weeks of serious focus. I'd never worked so hard on creations in my life.

Bella came in and plopped herself on my foot. I had made her a dog-sized traditional school uniform–style outfit: a red sweater with a matching red-and-black plaid skirt. I'd embellished it with sequins saying A+ all over it. I also attached a mini backpack made out of red velvet with plaid ribbons threaded through for straps.

So cute.

There was a knock on the door and my mom came in.

"Oh, I love that," my mom said, pointing to the prom dress. "I hate to interrupt you, but I wanted to let you know Shewz called. Their lawyers are finalizing the contract."

That should be good news. But seriously. The ad campaign was possibly the stupidest thing I'd ever seen in my life. And then what? I wouldn't let Shewz buy my idea? Yeah, right.

I looked at my mom, practically falling asleep standing up. I thought about Dex reminding me what we could do with some money around here and how my mom wouldn't have to work so much.

"Phabulous," I said. "With a P-H."

"You're not happy with the campaign, are you." My mom sat on my bed. Bella jumped up and sighed as my mom scratched her head.

"Well," I said, "that campaign is seriously painful."

"You could have spoken up," my mom said. "I think you should be honest with them, Lynn. You're their target audience *and* the shoe's creator. They should listen to you. And no matter what, you can back out anytime. I support you in whatever you choose."

"They did say they were doing some focus groups." I sighed. "So basically I'm hoping everyone tells them it's bad and they'll change some things."

Like *everything*.

31

And the big day arrived. The fashion show. I wanted to savor the moments before my first show, but it was not to be, with Chasey in charge.

"You better freaking hurry up and finish this," Chasey snapped. "The Shewz people just texted that they're on their way over. They said they have a surprise for us. It better be a big whomping contract for one of our models. They're getting restless."

Unfortunately there was no time to savor. In fact, there actually wasn't a lot worth savoring, since Chasey was stressing me out, and I still had to fit the models who were pacing around, waiting to be fitted into their clothes.

"It takes a while to get the clothes right," I hissed to Chasey as I pinned the back of her shirt to fit. "Okay, you're done."

Chasey went over to the mirror and, I have to say, it was

the first time I'd ever been happy to see her smile. I'd made an outfit for her that screamed school IT Girl. As much as I'd loved to have made her outfit inspired by, say, the cafeteria meat loaf or the girls' bathroom, I needed it to reflect her personality. I also needed to make the fashion show rock, so I couldn't sacrifice any of my outfits. She looked amazing in my creation.

"I need to go fix my makeup," she said. "I'll be back."

Right after Chasey walked out, Irene from Excelsiorama, Inc., walked in, wearing a charcoal suit and looking all business.

"Hi!" I said. "Welcome to the show!"

"Lynn, this is all so exciting," Irene said. "A great idea for this demographic. Eighty percent of tweens and teens report they want to attend a fashion show."

"Well, we sold a lot of tickets, so that's good," I said.

"I have something exciting to show you, so if you can take a little break," Irene said.

I was swamped with things to do, but of course I said yes.

"Here's the concept of the Shewz ad campaign for your shoe," she continued. "We're calling it: Phresh Phace. As I told you, we're going to introduce a new model with the campaign. Our new fresh face."

Right, that was where the IT panel came in. I could see them across the room, buzzing with excitement and competition.

"Wait until you see it," Irene said, and pulled out a mini-laptop. She held it up so I could see the screen. It said:

PhaB Pheet that Phunk presents:
Phresh Phace

Oh crud, they were using the *Ph*'s for *fresh face*, too. And then the screen dissolved into a new one.

"Who is that?" I asked, peering at the face of a gorgeous, supermodel-looking girl posing on the screen.

"Introducing . . . our fresh face!" Irene said dramatically. "And we brought her here for the show!"

I looked up as the girl on the screen appeared in real life and walked up to us, teetering on very high spiky heels.

"Hi!" the model squeaked. "I'm your Phresh Phace! I'm the model for your shoe campaign."

"What about the IT panel contest?" I asked cautiously.

"We rethought that," Irene said. "We believe girls are more likely to buy shoes worn by a top model rather than a regular girl. It's aspirational. They aspire to look like the model, although of course they never will."

Uh-oh, I didn't think Chasey and the IT panel were going to be happy about this new development.

"And here's the slogan for this ad." Irene showed me a new screen on the laptop.

Want to be IN?
Be IN like LIN!
Everyone kewl is wearing Shewz!

"And I'm Lin!" The model struck a pose.

"That's a coincidence. I'm Lynn, too," I said.

"Oh, it's no coincidence," Irene said brightly. "She's the new Lynn for our campaign!"

"Yes! It's me! I'm you!" the model squealed. "I'm the new you. Well, my name is really Josie, but *shh*, I'm pretending it's Lynn!"

"We wanted to stick with the story of a girl who created her own shoe, just like you," Irene explained. "But with our Lynn, we have a new, glamorous version of you that scored really high in our test market. We also changed the spelling of your name," she added. "We know that girls respond more to hipper names. So we changed it to Lin with an *i*. It scored higher in the focus groups."

I didn't know what to say. Or at least, I wasn't going to say what was going through my mind.

"But here's what we're most excited for you to see," Irene said. "Of course, it's not about the model or the spelling of the name. It's really about your shoe. And I'd like to present your Shoe! Click on the screen to see it!"

Irene clapped her hands with excitement as I clicked on the screen. And blinked when I saw what was on it. I looked at it again. It was a shoe. It resembled my shoe, but the pictures on it were very different. Instead of my creations and my photos, the shoe was covered with teddy bears and unicorns.

I looked closer. Little brown teddy bears with vacant staring eyes. And the unicorns were lime green with pink horns.

"Excuse me, but I don't think that's my shoe," I said, trying to be polite.

"Well, we tweaked it a little," Irene said. "But I assure you we did a lot of market research before we made any changes. Teddy bears and unicorns tested huge in our focus groups. So we made a few adjustments."

I stared at it again. That wasn't my shoe. I mean, I wanted individual styles and unique shoes. But not this!!! That wasn't anything I would create, much less wear. My head was buzzing. Phresh Phace? Teddy bears and lime green unicorns on my shoe? Everyone kewl is wearing Shewz? Being In like Lin?

"Who exactly was in your focus groups?" I asked.

"The boss's daughter and her friends," she said. "They're a little younger, but he said they're very sophisticated for elementary schoolers."

What?!?!

"This fashion show looks fabulous by the way," Irene said, looking around. "I'm so pleased we decided to write a big check for the charity tonight."

I closed my mouth.

"Hello!" Chasey suddenly appeared, and held out her hand charmingly. "I'm Chasey, coordinator of this event. But that doesn't mean I'm out of the running to be your Phresh Phace model!"

Well, actually, yes she was.

"And those are the other models," Chasey said brightly. She pointed, and all the girls smiled and waved back at us.

"They're perfectly darling," Irene said. "Lovely girls to represent your show. But wait. Oh dear, we can't have that."

I followed her gaze to Taylor, who was walking toward me, waving.

"That girl." Irene gestured at her, frowning. "That girl is wearing a knockoff of your shoe, Lynn."

"Oh, I made that for her," I said. "She's coordinating a lot of the show today."

"Oh, okay, a worker," Irene said. "You'll just want to make sure she stays behind the scenes. Or at least takes off her shoes."

I must have looked confused, because she went on, "Perhaps you're not quite understanding, dear," Irene said. "Shewz is going for an *aspirational* launch. Which means people like that girl are not the types we want to be wearing our shoe right now. It detracts."

I looked at Taylor, who was grinning and giving me a thumbs-up.

"Girls are going to want to copy you, and our Phresh Phace model, the faux Lynn," Irene continued. "And we're going to make a serious pitch to get Paris Hilton to wear your shoes and do something horribly embarrassing while the paparazzi take a picture of her!"

"Paris?" I said. "I don't know if my shoes are a Paris kind of thing."

"Good girl, you want to aim even higher," Irene said approvingly. "Let's shoot for the stars and get an actress.

Just as long as we stop girls lower down on the fashion food chain from wearing your shoe. Like *that*."

"THAT is my best friend, Taylor," I said.

"Don't worry, Irene," Chasey broke in. I didn't even realize she was still standing there. "I'll go tell Taylor to take off the shoes."

"No, you will not, Chasey. She can wear my shoe," I said firmly. I turned to Irene. "And so can any girl who wants to."

"Excuse us for a moment." Irene flashed a fake smile at Chasey and moved me off to the side. "I didn't mean to insult your friend, dear. It's just that this is big business and it's make it or break it time. Your shoe's getting some buzz now in some little online magazine. But face it, you can't let your shoes be worn by just anyone. Girls like that will ruin the image before you even launch."

My mind was racing. I thought of everything the Shewz campaign could bring our family. Then I thought of my dream of seeing my shoe in stores. But not like this.

"Remember the ad campaign," Irene said. "IN like LIN! Everyone *kewl* is wearing your shoe!! Emphasis on *kewl!*"

She looked pointedly at Taylor and grimaced.

"You know what"—I looked Irene in the eye—"I created the shoe because I was happy being me. Your ad campaign says the opposite. It doesn't matter who you are, just wear the shoe to be cool."

"Exactly!" said Irene happily. "Now she gets it!"

"Then I'm sorry," I said. "Thanks for thinking of me, but our deal just isn't going to work out."

"Excuse me? Now, now, don't be hasty," Irene said. "I know it's a stressful day for you. We could consider changing the spelling of your name back to Lynn, if that's a deal breaker."

"It's just the whole campaign is everything I'm not. Everything my shoe is not," I said.

"We did a lot of market research on this. You're making a big mistake here," Irene said frostily. "You do realize that your fifteen minutes of fame are almost over. In fact, the next IT Girl is about to debut on the *GlITter Girl* website, sixteen-year-old Hayley from Ohio. She makes things out of recycled materials. I'm sure she will be thrilled to hear from us about designing the new IT Shoe."

"I understand," I said. And I did.

"Ooh, that gives me a brilliant idea for future campaigns!" Irene muttered to herself. "Recycling! Reuse with Shewz! Trashy yet Sassy!"

I wondered if I should warn poor Hayley.

Irene went to the corner, pulled out her laptop, and started typing away.

"What's up with the Glamazon?" Chasey ran up to me, looking annoyed. She pointed to Lin, who was talking animatedly to the models. "I'm going to tell Taylor to seat that supermodel girl off to the side so she's out of view. She'll make me—I mean, our models—look bad."

I didn't even want to go there.

"She's with Shewz," I said. "But I think the Shewz people are leaving."

"Leaving? Where?" Chasey said. "Where are my sponsors going?"

No time to explain. I went over to Lin, with Chasey following behind.

"Hey, did you guys see where Irene went?" Lin/Josie asked. "Ooh, I love that." She pointed to the outfit Chasey was wearing. "Did you make that, Lynn? Can I wear those in the ad campaign?"

"Who are you?" Chasey asked her.

"I'm Lin!" she said cheerfully. "I'm the Phresh Phace of the new ad campaign for Shewz."

"They already picked their model?!" One of the models came up behind Chasey. "You said that WE were here to audition to be the Face of Lynn's Shewz campaign."

"Yeah, that's not working out so well. Anyway, I canceled the deal with Shewz," I said. "It's over. Sorry."

"You WHAT?" Chasey said. "Are you crazy? You are crazy. I always knew you were crazy. You dress crazy and you are crazy. I need to talk to Irene and stop your craziness."

Wow.

Chasey rushed over to Irene, followed by the models. I stayed put. I knew I was done with Shewz, and they were done with me. But I still had a fashion show to put on. I needed to focus on getting my outfits together. As I was sorting through the racks, Irene, Chasey, and the models came up to me.

"We had a change in plans," Irene said smoothly. "My new brilliant campaign idea will include some of the girls from the show."

"Great," I said. "I'm happy for all of you."

"Envision this!" Irene said gleefully. "Lin with an *i* will be in the middle of the ad page, wearing the shoe. And the slogan can be: REUSE WITH SHEWZ! Eco-friendly scores very high with our target demographic. And the regular girls will be tossing trash into the air all around. While we're here, I'll choose the models. Anyone who wants to audition for my new ad campaign, come with me to the main lobby."

"Wait, what? We have to do the fashion show!" I looked at Chasey, who was standing there in shock.

"Look, this is a chance at a real modeling job," one of the girls said.

And then the models started to walk away.

"Crud!" Chasey said. "I need to stop them. Plus, I need to make sure Irene chooses me as a model. I'll be back."

She ran after them.

Crud wasn't even remotely close to what I was thinking. I sank against the rack of clothes in disbelief. This was not going as planned. We were preparing to put on the very first Lynn Vincent fashion show. Apparently with no fashion models.

We had no models.

What do I do?

Lynn, I don't mean to interrupt your creative medita-tion, but people are starting to arrive, and I can't find the models," Taylor said.

I opened my eyes and lifted my head off my arms. I was slumped on the floor, behind one of the clothes racks.

"I'm not meditating," I said. "I've collapsed in horror. I don't know how to tell you this. There's not going to be a show."

I quickly filled Taylor in on what had just happened. I left out the part where Irene insulted her, though.

"So all the models left," I said. Taylor's mouth dropped open. "No models. No emcee. No show."

Taylor leaned against the wall. And slumped down next to me.

"But all your hard work," Taylor said.

"I know," I moaned.

"All your fans out there in the audience," Taylor said.

"I know," I moaned.

"The media," Taylor said, and then added, "A reporter from the newspaper is out there."

"You can stop now," I groaned.

"Lynn, you can't disappoint your fans," Taylor said.

"My fans are expecting to see a fashion show," I said. "And now we have no models. No sponsor. And no shoe deal. No college tuition. No car for Dex."

"Lynn, you needed to do what feels right," Taylor said. "It sounds like you did the right thing."

"Except we have no show," I said.

Grace ran up to us. "We're selling out! This place is packed. Taylor, there are some people who are looking for you. They said they're from the rec center?"

Oh no, the charity.

I put my head on my arms again.

"I'll go take care of them," Taylor said. "Lynn, don't do anything, okay? Give me just a couple minutes."

"Sure," I said gloomily.

Of course this was doomed to fail. What had I been thinking? I just felt bad for all the people who came out for a show. And for the rec center, since we'd have to give everyone their money back. I'd have to go out there and explain somehow. I felt the tears well up in my eyes. I'd always secretly daydreamed about having a fashion show when I was making my creations. I didn't even care it wasn't Paris or Milan or London or New York. Just having a fashion show in my own school cafeteria meant something special to me. All those times I'd sat in my closet even just a few months ago, dreaming about the day that people wouldn't laugh at me, at my clothes. . . .

"Did you ever think a few months ago when you sat in your closet making your clothes that you'd be putting on a sold-out fashion show?" a voice said above me.

No. No I—wait a minute. I wiped my eyes and looked up. And saw . . .

Valentyna.

I was definitely hallucinating. Chasey was right; I was going crazy. It seemed like Valentyna was in my school cafeteria, wearing a vanilla-colored jacket, full bronze skirt, and an emerald-and-gold chunky necklace.

"Valentyna?"

"Surprise, darling!" Valentyna reaching over to hug me. "I was in town, and of course I had to come stop by your very first fashion show."

"I can't believe you're here," I said. "This is amazing! Oh wait, it's not amazing."

"Don't worry, it's only natural for a designer to have the jitters before a show," Valentyna tried to reassure me.

"It's also natural for a fashion show to have models," I said. "Seriously, everything is going wrong."

I quickly explained about the Shewz fiasco.

"They wanted to buy my shoe and sell it," I said. "But I didn't agree with what they wanted to do with my shoe, so I told them no, and now I've messed up everything."

"Well, then," Valentyna said, "it sounds like you did the right thing. You stood by your values and you should feel proud of yourself for that. I knew we picked the right IT Girl."

"That's nice of you to say," I said miserably. "It all sounds good, but it's not working out so well for me."

Screwing up the fashion show and an opportunity to sell my shoe in stores. Maybe I could have talked them out of the campaign, at least the worst of it. And now Valentyna was here to witness this whole disaster.

"Lynn, since I'm here, I would love to see your collection," Valentyna said.

I sighed.

"Here they are," I said, trying to muster up some enthusiasm as we went over to the clothes racks. But before we could look at the clothes, we were interrupted.

"Lynn!" Taylor came running up to us and then slid to a halt.

"GLAH!" she choked. "Valentyna! Here! Glah!"

"Hello, I remember you," Valentyna said, smiling. "Lynn's friend who provided proof the shoe was hers. Nice to see you."

"You too," Taylor squeaked.

"Well, I'm happy to see one of your models came back," Valentyna said. "Now, which outfit is yours?"

"Omigosh, I'm so obviously not a model," Taylor said.

"Let me guess," Valentyna continued, and without missing a beat pulled out one of the outfits off the rack and motioned to Taylor. "This is the garment you're wearing today. Am I right?"

Valentyna looked at me with a raised eyebrow. And I got it.

"You are so right," I said.

I took it and I shoved the outfit into Taylor's hands.

"No time to waste," I said. "Go change. I can refit anything that needs it."

"What?" Taylor said. "What are you talking about?"

"Oh, before we dress the models, if I can impose," Valentyna said smoothly. "I have something that the crowd might enjoy while they're being seated. Do you like Justin Timberlake? I have his next song. It hasn't been released yet. I was given a preview copy, and I thought you could play it here."

She pulled a CD out of her huge bag and held it up.

"Eee! The new Justin Timberlake!" Taylor squealed.

"Why don't you give it to your DJ to play while we all finish getting ready?" Valentyna suggested. I was about to tell her we didn't have a DJ, but Taylor took the CD out of Valentyna's hands and ran off.

And then, as if things could get any weirder . . .

"I can so not believe this, Lynn." Chasey stomped up to us, fuming. "That Shewz woman didn't choose me for the ad. She said it was going to take her a while to narrow down the models, but I didn't need to bother staying. Me! And none of the other girls would leave with me. And did you see the audience? The front row filled up with people that are so not worthy of being front row people. I am not modeling today. I'm not emceeing. I refuse to be associated with this fiasco anymore."

"Okay," I said.

"What was I thinking? Like *you* could pull off my fashion show and—AUHHH!!" Chasey suddenly let out a scream. Then she just gaped.

"Valentyna, this is Chasey," I said. "Chasey, *the* Valentyna."

"Don't worry, Lynn," Valentyna said. "You run into temperamental models in this business. The show must go on without them. You can replace this one."

"Wait! What? You're here? I'm not being replaced!" Chasey stammered. "I—"

Valentyna ignored her. "I don't want to impose, Lynn, but if you would like me to help you fit the models into their clothes, I would be happy to help. I'd prefer less temperamental models than this one, though."

"I'll be good!" Chasey squeaked out. "You can fit me."

"Lynn, your mom said to tell you—" Grace came up and stopped in her tracks. Her mouth fell open when she saw Valentyna.

"I'll fit this one," Valentyna said, taking Grace's arm. "Now, doll, which outfit is yours?"

And it all fell into place.

"This one," I said, pulling out the most Grace-ish outfit.

"I'm ready! What do you think?" a voice called out. Arin Morgan stepped into the room. She was wearing the prom outfit, and she looked unbelievable.

"Lynn, I feel like a movie star," she said. "No, a princess."

"Nice work, Lynn." Valentyna smiled at me. "Stunning. I am impressed with your collection."

I smiled back. "I learned a few tricks from a mentor in her studio in New York City."

"I guess I'm ready early," Arin said. "Can I help with anything?"

"Are you willing to call some people and help me round up some models?" I asked her. I pulled out my cell phone and gave her the instructions of who to call. Valentyna took Grace and Taylor aside and started to fit the clothes on them. I smiled as I saw Taylor animatedly talking to Valentyna, and then Grace looking scared but excited as she held up her outfit.

I organized the clothes left on the racks, my mind racing with the possibilities. There was an excited buzz in the room.

I was going to have my first fashion show. I was going to make it happen. I smiled.

I wasn't smiling for long. After that, everything was chaos. Models were putting on their clothes, and Valentyna and I were doing our best to fit everyone quickly. Tweaks were made, wrinkles were smoothed, instructions were given.

"The audience is sitting down!" Chasey said. "It's almost time!"

"I need to get dressed," I said. "Oh, Valentyna! Guess what I'm wearing for the first time today? The dress we made together in New York."

"I was hoping you would," Valentyna said. "It's the perfect occasion. Now, since I have a bit of experience with fashion shows, would you like me to take the stage to introduce the show?"

"Wow," I said. "That would be huge."

Valentyna smiled and went over to make her entrance.

"I'm supposed to do that," Chasey snapped at me after Valentyna was out of earshot.

"Chasey, we have the opportunity to have Valentyna open our fashion show," I said. "Think about it."

"You're right, you're right," she admitted, surprising me. She did look disappointed, and for a moment I felt sorry for her.

"Plus, it will be awesome for you to make your appearance out on the runway as a model. So it's better this way. And, um, you look really, really good," I said.

Chasey brightened up, and I felt better. Plus it was true. Chasey looked incredible and reflected the purpose of the outfit well. That crisis averted, I took a deep breath and looked around. Everyone seemed as ready as they were going to be. I was as ready as I was going to be.

"Backstage, in your places," I said quietly. I grabbed the vintage cream heels with the giant buckles I'd attached to them and a cream-and-chocolate-colored beret. I slipped behind one of the changing stations and slid my New York City dress on. I looked down at the words to inspire me. And I ran my fingers over one of them. *Visible.*

Just as I was about to be. No matter what had happened—or would happen—this was my first fashion show. It was surreal. And we all filed into the backstage area to wait.

"Where's Taylor?" I asked Grace.

"She's fixing something last minute," Grace whispered. "She said she'll be right out."

I heard the music turn off, and the crowd quieted down. Then Valentyna's voice came over the speakers.

"Welcome, everyone." Valentyna's voice rang out into the auditorium. "I'm Valentyna."

The room filled with applause and gasps.

"One of my colleagues, Tom Ford, once said, 'When the youth of America gets together, amazing things happen,'" Valentyna said. "And I've had a sneak preview of this show, and I know you'll see that today. Once upon a very long time ago, I myself held my first fashion show. It is a moment to treasure. And now I'm so pleased to welcome you to a fashion show of the collection designed by your own local treasure. Your very own IT Girl's fashion show."

And here it was.

I heard music suddenly in the auditorium. And I heard loud cheering from the crowd as colored lights started beaming.

The models waited in line nervously as the song came to an end.

And then I heard the chant reverberate throughout the audience. "We want Lynn! We want Lynn!"

I took a deep breath. And I walked out onto the stage.

Valentyna kissed me on both cheeks and handed me the microphone. I looked out on the crowd from the stage. The lights were so bright, I could hardly see at first, but I could hear the cheers. The room looked packed.

"Wow," I said, my voice shaking. "Thank you, Valentyna. And thanks, everyone, for coming to the show. You're here for a great cause, the Community Rec Center."

A huge cheer went up from a corner of the auditorium. I squinted and saw a bunch of kids wearing red-and-white shirts with little stick people and the rec center logo on them.

And then the entire crowd started screaming wildly. I snapped out of it. What were they screaming at? I turned around. A giant movie screen was coming down behind me? And on the screen was—My Shoe!

The shoe that had started everything.

And then the music came back on. I looked up, and my jaw dropped as I saw who was in the DJ booth. My brother, apparently doing something techno-geeky with the movie screen. And Jacob, with DJ headphones on, apparently taking control of the music.

I took a deep breath.

"The theme of my fashion show is School Is My Runway," I said, trying to control my shaking voice. "My collection is about how school affects and inspires me. Valentyna reminded me that you might not always be appreciated everywhere, like, for example, your school. But it's important to stay true to yourself, even when it's not easy."

And suddenly a loud noise startled me, but then made me smile. The school bell was buzzing, just like it did between classes.

And I grinned and announced: "School is in session . . . Lynn-style!"

The lights dimmed. The music cranked up, and a spotlight shone on the stage, which we'd extended into a makeshift catwalk.

"The first day of school you want to make the right impression, and our first model definitely does. Here's Chasey, repping the first day of school in style," I announced.

Chasey walked out on the stage, and posed like a pro. Then she did a model walk down the long runway that led into the audience.

"Chasey is wearing plaid, but not the traditional school uniform," I said. "Back to school can be cool in this motorcycle-inspired cropped jacket with exposed zippers layered over a plaid T-shirt. She's wearing black pants with a wide leg and huge cuff at the bottom. And a long, soft, cream ruffled cashmere scarf to add some dimension and a luxurious feel to start the school year off right."

I had to give Chasey props for working the crowd and my outfit.

"Chasey put a lot of time into this show," I said. "Thanks, Chasey!"

The audience cheered; some flashbulbs went off. Jacob hit the class-changing school bell again as Chasey swished out.

"Where's the first place you go when you get to school?" I asked the crowd. "Your locker! The next outfit is inspired by your school locker and is worn by Marissa."

And the female half of the Makeout Couple came out on the runway, blowing a kiss to her boyfriend.

"Marissa is wearing a silvery gray cotton twill top representing the shiny gray of the locker. The silver chains are pinned off it, with a bracelet made out of a combination lock. Her silvery gray A-line skirt is made of squares of different fabrics—silk, bouclé, wool—each to provide a different texture and shine."

The school bell rang to switch models, and then Grace came out. And Grace really came out of her shell as she walked tall and out onto the stage and down the runway. She had her hair pulled into an updo, with #2 pencils sticking out of the bun.

"Grace is one of those people who actually like the

school part of school, so she looks like Superstudent in a very tailored, buttoned-up, long black bouclé jacket that hits just a few inches above her knee, accented with bold red stitching.

"Grace is a serious student, but she also knows how to have fun, as shown by the peacock feathers coming out of the sleeve opening, under the cuff, and at the bottom of the jacket. She's wearing a white pleated skirt and above-the-knee fishnet hose because, well, I thought it looked good. And I wanted to call attention to her shoes, which are painted with chalkboard paint so you can write all over them."

Grace waved and went backstage. Jacob hit the school buzzer and switched to a more indie rock song as Char came out next.

"Char is a stylistic mash-up that represents those of us who don't really feel like they always fit in at school. But it's a tribute to keeping your creativity and being comfortable with who you really are.

"She's wearing loose-fitting dark navy jeans that are destroyed. On the denim I bleached out stripes for a faded-white look, and for a touch of pretty I laced ribbon up the side of the jeans. They are topped off with a pretty sleeveless tank made of a silk cream charmeuse with strips of fabric loops, so it looks like bubbles are going down the front and around the neckline."

I couldn't help but notice that Char worked the catwalk like nobody's business.

"Work it, Char," I said, and she grinned at me as she exited the stage.

The crowd went wild when Arin came out in her dress. She glowed.

"Arin is going to the prom, and her dress was inspired by Old Hollywood glamour."

I described the dress as Arin doing what she did so well: look and act like a princess with grace and with class.

"And now, the last day of school," I said. The school bell buzzed, and I waited for Taylor. But then I saw Grace frantically waving at me from offstage.

"Let's give some applause to our DJ, Jacob," I said. Jacob turned up the music and I walked backstage as if it were planned.

But it wasn't.

"Where's Taylor?" I raced back and asked the group of models waiting back there.

"Stage fright. We can't get her to do it," Grace said, pointing to Taylor, who was pacing in the corner. She lowered her voice. "Taylor said people will laugh at the thought of her being a model."

I marched over to Taylor.

"Taylor," I said to her. "You've got to go on. You look amazing, I swear. Just be free and have fun and go for it for once."

"I can't," she said. "I'm sorry, but just finish without me. It works out perfect that Arin closes the show."

"Taylor," I said, "remember when you used to say you

were tired of being invisible? I want you to go out there and be, well . . ."

I pointed to the word on the front of my dress: *Visible*.

"This means something to me," I said. "And it means a lot that you're in my show."

"I'm sorry," Taylor said. "I know you're my best friend, so you have to put me in this to be nice, but I . . . I just can't."

"Taylor," a voice boomed behind me. I turned around and saw Valentyna in full fashion-designer diva pose. "I am not your best friend, so I'm not just being nice. I fitted you myself, and I want you out on the stage in that incredible outfit."

"But—" Taylor protested.

"I have dealt with many temperamental models in the past, and not one dared to challenge me twice." Valentyna looked her in the eye. "Now, GO."

Taylor's eyes widened, but she scurried to the edge of the stage.

I flashed Valentyna a look of gratitude and quickly went back out onto the stage, where Jacob was entertaining the crowd with a remix as Dex did a strobe-light show out into the audience. Jacob gave me the thumbs-up and lowered the music when he saw me reenter.

"And now, for the grand finale of the first ever school fashion show . . ." I announced. "Celebrating the last day of school is Taylor!"

Taylor came out onstage, tentatively. The music switched back to the sneak preview Justin Timberlake dance song, now remixed. She looked a little panicky but started her walk toward the audience.

"This outfit was inspired by the feeling of freedom and fun of the last day of school, but also how I want people to feel when they wear my clothes," I said. "I get dressed every day like it's a celebration. Taylor is wearing a full short skirt made of red taffeta. Her jacket is made of red canvas—yes, it's fabric from a real backpack. I used the back backpack straps as the straps of the shirt, and the zipper up the front. And along the bottom of the skirt you can see black-and-white photos printed—faces from our very own school's yearbook."

Along the hem of the skirt I'd written the kinds of things you'd write in a yearbook like: *Had so much fun with you this year! Friends forever! Love ya!*

I paused and let Taylor have a moment in the spotlight. I thought about all those times she felt fashion had let her down, depressed and confused her. I wanted her to enjoy it tonight.

"Valentyna reminded me that everyone should feel happy, confident, and truly themselves in their clothes. And tonight, especially Taylor, because Taylor is the most caring person I know and she deserves to feel that way. I mean, it's because of her we've raised more than twelve hundred dollars for the rec center tonight. Taylor is a great combination of fashion and compassion."

Taylor waved at the audience, and then she suddenly

beamed. I saw where she was smiling, and it was at her mom. Mrs. Snyder was beaming, too. And heh, she was sitting next to Mrs. Welch, who was clapping as well.

"I love being the *GlITter Girl* IT Girl," I said. "But what I really love is to see people happy in my creations."

Then the school bell rang, and all the models filed back onto the runway in a group, behind me.

And I stood there, in the dress I'd created with Valentyna, as my very first fashion show was ending. And I started to tear up, as all my nerves burst out of me. Taylor squeezed my hand, and I took a deep breath to finish.

"Valentyna told me that the best fashion comes from your heart and reflects the true you. I first learned that when I made a shoe."

I turned around and pointed to the picture of my shoe on the screen.

"That is the shoe that started it all," I said. "And I want to invite you all to stop by and celebrate after the show with me at FonDo. Thank you for coming."

Jacob cranked up the music and I walked offstage. And I heard a lot of applause.

We were sitting in our usual table at the back of Fon-Do. It was a little more crowded than usual, so we'd pulled up extra chairs.

"This is our usual table," I said to Valentyna. "It's a little noisy, but it's ours."

It was pretty wild to be sitting with Valentyna at Fon-Do, along with Taylor, Grace, my mom. And my Bella, who was nestled on the floor next to me, wearing her fashion show outfit.

I had changed out of my fashion show outfit so I wouldn't get fondue on my special dress. I was wearing a red-and-white rec center volunteer T-shirt with the stick figures on the front that the kids had given me after the show. I had it on with the white pleated skirt Grace had worn in the fashion show, and the red canvas jacket Taylor had worn. And my own kneesocks—the ones that had unraveled the first time I was here at FonDo.

And of course, The Shoe.

"The bubble tea is really good," Taylor suggested to Valentyna. "Here comes the waiter."

Dex came over, but he wasn't in waiter mode.

"Jett will be your server today," Dex announced, pointing to a guy cleaning a table. "I was promoted to assistant manager after I helped them install a new high-tech cash register that reduces human error by twenty-two and a half percent."

"Congrats, Dex," I said.

"At this rate, I will have a car in less than a month." Dex grinned.

"Dex, sign my T-shirt?" I pulled the red jacket off and turned around so he could sign the back of the shirt. It was covered in signatures of people from the show tonight. There was Valentyna, Grace, Kate, Arin, the Makeout Couple, my mom. Ooh, the shirt would look really cute if I cut the neckline into a V and then—

"Hello? Earth to Lynn? Hand over the pen?" Dex was holding out his hand. Oh! I gave him the pen.

Dex took the permanent marker and signed his name on the side. He slid into a chair next to my mom.

"Valentyna gave me some great advice today while she was fitting me and I was telling her how I pretty much was hating fashion because it stressed me out," Taylor said happily.

"In the words of fashion designer Donatella Versace: 'Fashion is all about happiness. It's fun. It's important. But it's not medicine,'" Valentyna quoted.

"Well, tonight I definitely had fun with the fashion." Taylor grinned. "Thanks, Valentyna, for getting my butt out there on the stage. I was more scared to say no to you than to do it!"

"And thank you for my flowers," I said, patting the bouquet of white calla lilies Valentyna had given me at the end of the show. "Thank you for everything."

"Valentyna, what made you come into town?" my mom asked Valentyna.

"I'm here for my best friend's anniversary party," Valentyna said.

"You have a friend who lives here?" I asked her.

"Not only that, but family here, too. Didn't you ever wonder why I set the first IT Girl search here in this town?" Valentyna asked.

"Yes, of course," I said. "I mean, this is not the first place you think of to discover anything in fashion."

"Ah, but I do." Valentyna smiled. "I grew up here."

"You did?" everyone gasped.

"I was once Valerie Grubb," Valentyna said. "I used to come to this very place after school when it was the ice-cream parlor. I wore clothes that everyone thought were bizarre. Nobody but my best friend understood me at all. After high school I moved to New York, changed my name, got a job in fashion, and voilà!"

"I can totally relate to that," I said, elbowing Taylor. "The whole nobody but my best friend understood me part, anyway."

"So, you went off to the city and became famous in fashion but you're still friends with your friend from home?" Taylor asked.

"Yes," Valentyna said. "And she lives here in a cozy house, with her three lovely children and her loving husband. And she is very happy. And we are still best friends."

"Whew!" Taylor said, sounding relieved. "Did you hear that, Lynn?"

I hadn't realized she even worried about that.

"Now, Lynn, ask me who that best friend is," Valentina said.

"Um, who's your best friend?" I asked.

"She happens to be the head of admissions at the art school a few towns over," Valentyna said. "And I told her about a young person who would be an ideal candidate for her Saturday-morning fashion design classes."

"She means you, Lynn!" Taylor squealed.

"Mom?" I looked at my mother.

"Oh, and there's a scholarship involved," Valentyna said. "It will be free."

"And Dex could drive me in his new car!" I said.

"I could what?" Dex said. "Hey, wait a minute—"

"I heard that art school has a great photograph gallery," Arin said. "Maybe I could tag along sometimes and we could go see it together, Dex."

"Uh, yeah!" Dex said, his voice sounding strangled. "Definitely. That sounds great. My GPS will get us there, no problem."

Oh, Dex.

"And while you're doing that, I'll have my Saturday-morning activity," Taylor said.

"Your round-off cartwheel classes?" I asked.

"Nope," Taylor said cheerfully. "After my mother saw me as a model onstage with everyone cheering, she softened. You made one of her dreams come true, so she's letting me have one of my dreams. I'm going to volunteer at the rec center on Saturdays."

"Awesome!" I said.

"Well, that's a worthwhile cause," my mother told her.

"I'm surprised your mom isn't making you take any more lessons," I said.

"Please, it's my mother we're talking about," Taylor said. "Of course she is. But now it will be only once a week. She still thinks I'm trying out for cheerleading this spring."

"I'm having horrible flashbacks," Valentyna said. "My own mother wanted me to be a cheerleader. So I wore these horrible brown corduroy pants and a bright yellow shirt to cheerleading tryouts to scare off the judges. It worked. I didn't even have to humiliate myself with my lack of coordination before I was dismissed."

"Ooh, I might have to try that," Taylor said. "Thanks for the tip."

Just then my cell started buzzing with a text message.

Lynn, thank you for e-mailing the pictures from your fashion show. We're interested in doing a follow-up story on GlITter Girl Online about your show. Will be in touch.

Whitney

"Pictures from the fashion show?" I said. "How did Whitney get pictures of the fashion show?"

"Oh, I can't imagine," Valentyna said, casually pulling out her iPhone and holding it so I could see it was on the camera app. "You must have had a photographer at the show. Looks like you will have more than just fifteen minutes of fame, Lynn. And now, I must leave. My friend's anniversary party awaits. I hope to see you in New York soon."

"That could be a good spring break trip," my mom said, sipping her bubble tea.

This is so great.

"Farewell," Valentyna said. She gave me a double-cheek kiss good-bye.

"Thank you so much for everything," I said to her.

So many people had come through today for the show. I'd pretty much gotten to thank everyone. But there was one person I hadn't gotten to thank, and he was walking in the front door of FonDo.

"That guy totally saved the music." Dex tilted his head toward Jacob. "That girl Chasey had some awful pop princess stuff planned."

"I need to go thank him," I said. Jacob was high-fiving

one of the guys at the front table. "I'll be right back."

I walked up to the front of the place.

"Hey," I said. "I just wanted to thank you for being the DJ. I hear you saved the music."

"Well, kicking it off with the new Justin song made it pretty easy," he said. "Where did you get that? No wait, you're the IT Girl, of course you get the new music."

"Not usually," I laughed.

"The show was great," he said. "I really liked you."

"Thanks," I said. And then we both realized what he said.

I laughed. "Don't worry. I know you meant you really liked the show."

"Yeah," he said. "That's what I meant. Well, you know I like *you*, so obviously I meant the show. Okay, I'm embarrassing myself."

"What do you mean I know you like me?" I asked, confused.

"You know I like you," he said.

I shook my head. *No.*

"Uh, trying to kiss someone is usually a pretty good clue?" he said.

"Wait. You *were* trying to kiss me?" I said. "You mean that day at the locker?

"Yeah, and then you looked horrified and pulled away?" he said. "So, you knew I liked you. You didn't like me back. I mean, I get why. I knew it was stupid of me to even think you'd like me back."

"What? Why?" My head was spinning.

"I knew you wouldn't really like someone like me. I'm too average. You'd like someone cooler and more interesting."

"Hello? You are cool and interesting," I said. "You DJ. You knit. You're smart. You wear cool retro green shoes—"

"Shut up and kiss already," someone called out.

We both jumped. It was the guy from Makeout Couple. He and his girlfriend were in a nearby booth, giving me a thumbs-up.

I felt my face turning bright red. But I looked Jacob straight in the eye.

"You're definitely not average," I said. "And I didn't mean to pull away or look at you in horror. See, I'd accidentally glued my head to the locker and—"

Jacob looked at me for a second and then, thankfully, he interrupted me.

"Maybe you should just stop that explanation there. I don't think I want to know."

"No, you don't," I agreed. "So wait. You really wanted to kiss me?"

"I still want to. So this is a test. If you jump away this time or look horrified . . ." He didn't finish the sentence, but motioned toward the back door. I followed him to the back and out the door to the area behind the Dumpster.

"It's not glamorous, but it's private," Jacob said. "I want to ask you something. Do you—"

"Lynn!" Chasey's sneering voice made me jump again. "I know you're back here."

Chasey stuck her head around the Dumpster, and she gasped.

"Oh, Jacob's here! I'm not interrupting anything, am I? Ha-ha." Her voice was all supersweet now.

"Actually, yes you are," Jacob said.

Chasey stopped laughing.

"Uh . . . uh . . . I just thought Lynn might want this," Chasey said. She held up a long piece of yarn. "I found it stuck on the back door of FonDo. So, uh. I knew where you were because I followed the trail."

And then I felt a tug. I looked down. The other end of the yarn was attached to something—my leg. One of my socks had unraveled.

"So. Okay, bye," Chasey said, backing away. I'd never seen her face turn red before. It was an unflattering shade of red, too; it clashed with her hair. "But wait! Lynn, do you know if Valentyna is still here?"

"Oh, you just missed her," I said. "So sorry."

"Good-bye," Jacob said firmly.

Chasey dropped the yarn and fled.

"I seriously need to learn how to knit better," I said, gathering the yarn off the ground into a little ball.

"I know a good teacher," Jacob said. "Maybe we can take knitting classes with my grandmother. And then go to a movie or out to dinner or . . . I'll just spit it out. Do you want to go out with me?"

I looked at him, standing behind a Dumpster and holding my yarn in his hand. Looking very cute.

"Yes," I said. "Yes, I want to go out with you."

"Great!" Jacob said. "Okay! We're going out. Okay! So. We should probably get back in there, since you're celebrating and all."

And then he took my hand. Jacob didn't let go of my hand as we walked toward the door and inside FonDo. Holding hands.

As we were walking to my table, I heard someone call out my name.

I turned around to see a girl I vaguely recognized from one of my classes. She was wearing a shirt with a painted peace sign on it, I noticed.

"Omigosh," she said, looking at us holding hands. "I didn't know Lynn had a boyfriend. You're so lucky you have Lynn as your girlfriend."

"I know," Jacob said. He looked at me and smiled as I blushed.

"Lynn, can I ask you a personal question?" the girl asked me.

"Hey, how about I go say hi to your mom and everyone," Jacob said.

"Cool," I said. "I'll be right there."

"Lynn, I wanted to tell you I'm a huge fan of yours," the girl said. "I loved your show."

"Thanks," I said. "That's really nice to hear."

"I wanted to ask you which one would look best on me. I took pictures at the fashion show so I can copy all of your outfits," she said, holding up a camera phone. "I'm adding them to the ones I took at school."

"You know what," I said. "You're not supposed to copy me. Your style is supposed to be your own."

And then I had an idea.

"I'll make you a trade," I said. "If you can e-mail me the pictures you took from the show, I'll help you make something that's just for you."

"Really?" she said. "Yes!"

The girl smiled as I plugged my number into her cell. And I smiled as I quickly flipped through the pictures she took of the show. Valentyna. Grace. Arin. Hey, there was Jacob DJ-ing. Even Dex. And Taylor, in the grand finale.

Yup, I knew exactly what I was going to do with these pictures. I was going to shrink them and collage them. I had a shoe that needed a match at home. I was going to make The Shoe Part 2. And ooh! A bag. I'd make a new IT bag that would go with The Shoe! *A brocade clutch,* I thought as I walked to the back of FonDo. *No, a slouchy big bag with room for yarn and sewing supplies. Dark plum and gold? A pistachio green with tangerine accents? Or a more cheery turquoise blue or blossom yellow, to reflect my happiness at this moment—*

I suddenly realized I was standing in the back of FonDo, spacing out. And people were looking at me. I remembered the first day I came to FonDo and how people had stared at me. I remembered my first-day-of-school goals of getting through the year without a public humiliation and having somewhere to sit at lunch. And how I was humiliated my first day in FonDo when my sock first unraveled.

"That's Lynn," I heard someone say. "She's the *GlITter*

Girl IT Girl! Look, she's thinking about something. Do you think there's something here that's inspiring her?"

"Here? What could be inspiring *here*?" her friend replied.

I looked toward where my family and friends were waiting for me at our table and smiled.

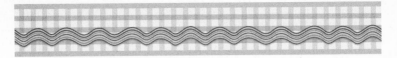

Writing a book is not DIY and I am grateful to be surrounded by an inspiring and creative team.

· · · · · · · · · · · · · **Thanks to:** · · · · · · · · · · · · ·

☆ Dave, Jack, and Quinny DeVillers;

☆ Jennifer Lynn Rozines Roy, who brainstormed the original idea for Lynn with me;

☆ Leah Purcell, my high school friend who was the original inspiration for Lynn;

☆ Whitney Jerwers, Joe Williams at Justice, Kait Feldman, Robin Rozines, Amy Rozines, Tavi;

☆ Polyvore.com, for sponsoring a contest for people to design some of the outfits Lynn wore! Congrats to contest winners: Emily Liz, Marifer, Lucy, "Painthead," and Wanda;

☆ Julie Strauss-Gabel, my brilliant and creative editor. And to everyone else at Dutton, especially Lisa Yoskowitz, Kristin Smith, and Jason Henry.

☆ Mel Berger, my über-agent at William Morris Endeavor; and Lauren Heller Whitney, Julie Colbert, Anne-Elise Schaffir, and Anna DeRoy at WME;

☆ and to all of my readers.

☆ And in memory of Lynne Hartunian, another "Lynn" with her own wonderful style.

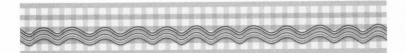